The Fool Stories

Book Two

Dreaming of Dreams

Dr. Jessica Hart
Illustrated by Margot J. Ott

Words of Wizdom
International, Inc.
Miami Beach · Florida

Illustrator: Margot Janet Ott
Text Design: J. Stone, Ph.D.
Editor: Leslie Weld
Type Selection: Alexander Kohlrautz
Cover Design: Jonathan Pennell
Manufactured in China
First Printing

ISBN: 1-884695-17-5

The Library of Congress CIP Date for all books in The Fool Stories series is:

Library of Congress Cataloging-in-Publication Data

Hart, Jessica, 1952-
        The Fool stories / Jessica Hart ; illustrated by Brian Keeler.
        p.   cm.
        Contents: Bk. 1. The adventure begins
        Summary: The Fool, a travelling storyteller, meets people,
animals, and extraterrestrial beings on his journeys and shares his
tales with them.
        ISBN 1-884695-09-4 (v. 1) : $18.95 ($25.50 Can.)
        [1. Storytelling--Fiction.]   I. Keeler, Brian, 1953- ill.
II. Title.
PZ7.H25684Fo   1994
[Fic]--dc20   94-46925
                                                                        CIP
                                                                         AC

Dedicated to:

All the big people, and all the little people,
in the whole wide world.

Other titles in this series:

The Fool Stories, Book One, The Adventure Begins

The Fool Stories: Book Two
Dreaming of Dreams

Table of Contents

Fool's Dream: Number One

Where Fool becomes a sand crab, escapes from a storm
and hears a new story.

Sparkling snowflakes fell silently from heaven, covering the forest with a thick, heavy blanket. Like Grandmother Hattie's Blankets of White Light, it calmed and quieted noise, fear, and worry. Under the safe, dark veil of winter, the forest and her creatures slept peacefully. In a small, dry cave, well-hidden behind the branch of a shaggy fir tree, Fool, his fluffy yellow dog, Intuit, and their dear friend, an old brown bear, cuddled together, snoring and dreaming sweet dreams.

Sleeping close to his two furry friends, Fool felt their comforting warmth. In a dream, he recalled the feeling of stretching out on a little peninsula where he and Intuit had rested after a most exciting boat ride. Tired from the thrill of speeding down a rushing river in a tiny, green rowboat, the two friends had taken afternoon naps. Now, in his sleep, Fool felt warm sand on his cheeks, and he began to melt into the sandy beach. Melting down, down, down he became smaller and smaller. At the same time, the grains of golden sand began to grow bigger and bigger and bigger, until finally, they looked like rocks the size of golf balls.

"Hey!" he shouted with a tiny squeak, "what's going on?" Spinning around, he noticed that his hands, or rather what used to be his hands, had turned into strange, claw-like things. They were a pale, sandy color, almost clear. "What? What?" Looking down, he realized his whole body had changed! Instead of two legs wearing brown tights and green shorts, he now had eight very skinny legs with knobby knees. His body, disk-shaped and almost flat, certainly didn't resemble anything he recognized! Panic-stricken, he shouted, "What's happened to me?"

9

"Whaddaya mean, what's happened to you?" piped up an equally squeaky voice behind him. Suddenly, without warning, a huge mound of sand fell on top of Fool, covering him completely. Sputtering and spitting, Fool instinctively began using his newly formed claws to dig at the sand. In an instant, he'd dug himself out from under the sand, leaving behind a neat little tunnel.

"Darned dog!" complained the voice he'd heard before. As Fool tried to turn around to see the speaker, he first felt his legs scurry sideways away from the voice, then, having traveled in a big circle, he scampered back toward the voice. Totally amazed, Fool pondered this entirely new way of moving.

"Can you believe those dogs! Always stepping on our tunnels!" Fool found himself face to face with a very pale, flat creature with eight skinny legs, eight knobby knees, and two huge, scoop-like claws. The most interesting features were two roving, jet black eyes sticking up on the ends of long antennae attached smack atop the creature's round body.

"What are you?" asked Fool, not knowing if he should laugh at the creature, or run away in fear.

"What do you mean, 'what are you?'" the creature scoffed. "I'm a sand crab, just like you. What a question! That dog must have stepped on your brain!"

"I'm... I'm a sand crab?" Fool whistled low in amazement. "Wow!"

"And from the way you're talking, I'd say you're a pretty strange sand crab too!" hurrumphed the other. "My name's Stanley. Are you new to this beach?"

Without waiting for an answer, Stanley scuttled very, very quickly sideways across the beach and snapped at a fly resting on the ground close to the water's edge. Missing the fly, the crab made a clicking sound and skittered sideways back to Fool leaving tiny v-shaped tracks as he ran.

"Don't just stand there, do something! We sand crabs are always doing something! We're never still. Move, move!"

"What should I do?" whimpered Fool, not at all sure he enjoyed being a sand crab.

"Why dig, of course!" shouted the other crab, flinging clawfuls of soft white sand into the air. Faster and faster he dug until he began to disappear into a deep tunnel. Every few seconds he scurried out of the tunnel, peered about, flung scoops of sand into the air, then dropped back down the tunnel out of sight.

"Well, okay," thought Fool. "I guess if I am a sand crab, I may as well act like a sand crab." Beginning to dig, he found the work actually quite enjoyable, and soon he was disappearing into a neat little tunnel of his own making. Coming to the surface to toss a clawful of sand, he spied a tiny bug crawling toward his hole.

Without even thinking, Fool's eight legs scrambled out of the hole and, with amazing speed, skittered across the beach toward the bug. Startled, the bug jetted in the opposite direction with Fool racing behind him. Busy with the chase, Fool didn't notice the heavy storm clouds rolling across the darkening sky.

KABOOM! Thunder split the air with a tremendous crash, frightening Fool so much that he got tangled in his own legs and went tumbling over and over in the soft sand. Seeing an opportunity to escape becoming a sand crab's dinner, the bug hurried off to hide under a round, orange shell. Confused and frightened, Fool forgot all about the bug.

KABOOM! Thunder clapped through the heavens. This time, thick plops of heavy rain accompanied the sound. Each drop felt like a giant stone crashing onto Fool's tender body. "Ouch! Ouch!" he cried, dashing sideways back to his newly dug tunnel.

"Oh, no! Not again!" Finding his tunnel covered over by the footprint of a large dog, Fool collapsed on the sand, crumpling his eight knobby knees beneath him.

"What is it now?" shouted Stanley, scurrying by to pop into yet another newly dug hole. Sliding down his tunnel he grabbed two clawfuls of sand and scrambled up again. "Why are you crying? Normal sand crabs are simply too busy to cry!" he said disgustedly.

"It's just that, I'm not really sure about being a sand crab. And... and," Fool sniffled, "it's starting to rain, and my hole got squished in and, and..." he began to cry loudly.

"Shhh!" scolded Stanley. Peering sideways at Fool through his bobbing eyes, he softened a bit. "Oh, very well, then," he muttered, tossing a final clawful of sand out of his latest tunnel. "Come with me into my new hole. You'll be safe during the storm. I'll tell you a story I heard while watching humans at one of their beach parties."

"A story?" sniffled Fool, brightening a bit.

"Oh, yes," answered Stanley, puffing out his tiny chest. "We sand crabs know a great deal more than we're given credit for! We see and hear just about everything that happens on the entire beach. We have quite a few stories, if I do say so! Hurry!" Waving one claw at Fool he quickly backed into his tunnel.

CRACK! A blazing streak of lightning flashed across the sky. Jumping sideways, Fool tumbled antenna over claws into Stanley's tunnel.

Finding the hole to be quite dry and cozy, Fool stopped whimpering and relaxed. Stanley continued moving constantly, digging a bit of sand here, tossing a few grains of sand over there, never pausing. As he rearranged the structure of his hole, he shared the story he'd heard just a few nights before. This is the story Fool learned from Stanley, the sand crab, as they sat out the raging summer storm.

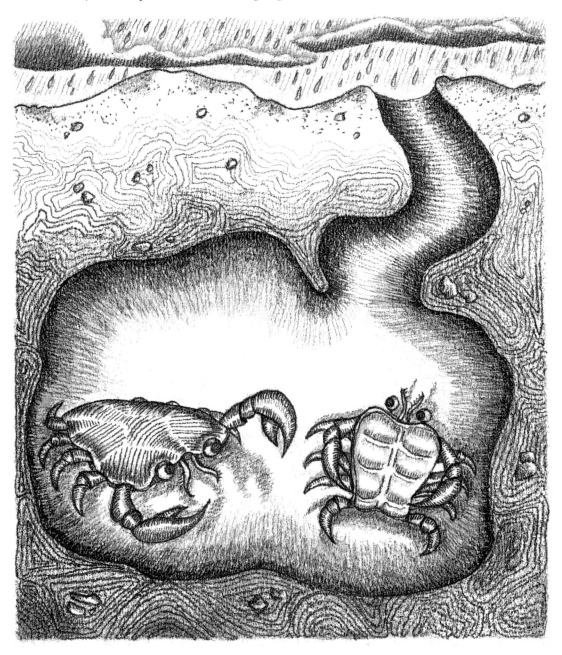

Clyde Thomas

and

The Magic Mirror

Chapter One

<u>Clyde Thomas and the Magic Mirror</u>

SPLASH! Clyde Thomas landed with both feet directly in the middle of a large, salty puddle.

"Hey, boy! Slow down! You gittin' me all wet!" Uncle Frazier laughed at Clyde Thomas as the young boy raced from puddle to puddle, jumping high, creating a spray of sea water each time he landed.

Uncle Frazier's rich dark brown skin glistened like the shiny wings of little beetles scampering up coconut trees. His midnight black hair hung down to his waist in thick, curling dredlocks. Smelling of patchouli and musk, he swayed as he moved his tall, thin body down the beach. Uncle Frazier, a handsome Rastafarian, was Clyde Thomas' favorite friend.

"Better git outta da way den!" yelled Clyde Thomas, imitating his friend's language. Racing toward another pool, and flashing a big smile, Clyde Thomas' bright, white teeth lit up his dark face. His thin brown arms, flapping in the air, looked like palm fronds tossing in the wind.

Living on a small island in the middle of the Caribbean with his mother and Uncle Frazier, Clyde Thomas was used to lovely, sun-drenched days. Warm and sparkley, the turquoise water around his island was so clear that Clyde Thomas and his friends could see all the way down to the sandy bottom. At least, they could most of the time. But after big storms, the water turned a deep, dark green. Those storms caused the schools to close because heavy rains turned the island roads to chocolate milk. No one could drive cars or run the school bus on the muddy roads, so Clyde Thomas and all the other island children had

time off from their school lessons. Clyde Thomas loved the days following big storms.

People living on Clyde Thomas' island viewed tropical storms as both scary and exciting. Some storms simply blew dust and mist off the island, leaving everything green, fresh, and shiny. These storms were gentle and tender. During stronger storms, however, great, fierce winds whipped around, stirring the angry ocean. Huge waves reared up, covered with white foam that resembled the manes of angry horses. Sometimes the winds swept straight across the ocean and traveled right up onto the island, blowing down trees, houses and, once, even the steeple of the Methodist church. When the waves were really big, and the wind was especially fierce, the storm stole chairs, toys, clothes hanging from lines, and many other possessions of the islanders and carried them far out across the ocean, never to be seen again. But when the ocean washed things off the island, it returned wonderful surprises. After a storm, the beaches around the island would be littered with these things. Huge tree trunks (roots and all), shells, bottles and cans. Fishing nets, lobster traps, buoys and even an occasional broken boat motor, all found themselves tossed onto the land.

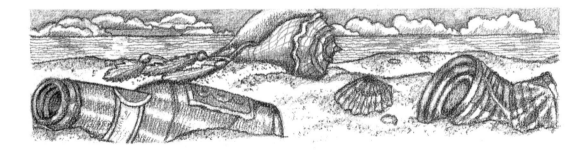

Uncle Frazier had explained to Clyde Thomas and his sister Siri, that the ocean gives and the ocean takes away. All a person has to do is seek the treasures the ocean offers. One time, Uncle Frazier discovered a very old Spanish coin the ocean dropped on the beach. A white man visiting the island offered $400.00 for the coin. But Uncle Frazier kept it because the ocean had given him the coin as a gift.

Another time Uncle Frazier found a fashion doll for Siri. The doll's hair and eyes were bleached completely white by the salt water. But mother fixed the doll by using nail polish to paint bright red lips and deep burgundy eyes. Carefully gluing a large mat of dog fur to the doll's head she created thick, fluffy hair. Clyde Thomas thought the doll was very silly looking, but Siri loved her gift from the ocean.

Today, a clear and beautiful day, following yesterday's very big storm, Clyde Thomas had the feeling he would receive a special gift from the ocean. Running down the beach treasure hunting with Uncle Frazier, he splashed in puddles and skipped in and out of small, dark green waves at the water's edge, laughing and squealing each time one of them sprayed him. Uncle Frazier kept a steady pace, slowly and rhythmically zig zagging across the beach, head down, eyes scanning the sandy shore.

SPLAT! Clyde Thomas landed both feet flat in a deep pool. Shooting up like a fountain all around him, the water drenched his already damp pants and shirt.

"Yea!" he yelled at the top of his lungs, running farther along the beach. Just as he was about to make a second giant leap into an even larger puddle, he noticed something peeking out from a mound of stringy spinach-like seaweed. "Hey, mon," he wondered out loud, "what's this?" Using a stick to clear away the gummy plant, he found a small, pink plastic mirror. Wiping the mirror clean with the hem of his shirt, Clyde Thomas saw a happy, brown-skinned boy grinning back at him. "Girl stuff," he thought, cramming the mirror into the back pocket of his shorts.

"C'mon boy!" Uncle Frazier shouted from down the beach. "It's time for you to come on home for lunch, you know."

"Coming!" replied Clyde Thomas, leaping into a nearby puddle and making a waterfall as he landed.

After lunch, Clyde Thomas slid the mirror under the school

clothes in his dresser drawer and skipped outdoors to play with his friends in the chocolate milk roads. Clyde Thomas forgot about the mirror, his gift from the ocean, until, after falling asleep that night, he had the most peculiar dream he could ever remember.

Holding the mirror, he found himself standing in a strange place that had no visible walls, no ceiling, and no floor. Walking slowly, from nowhere at all, a man dressed in the official post office uniform worn by mail carriers on the island, approached Clyde Thomas. Before Clyde Thomas could say a word, the man spoke and introduced himself.

"Hello, Clyde Thomas. My name is Ralph. I'm the Angel of Childhood Dreams. I see you've got yourself a new mirror. What sort of magic have you been seein' lately?"

Clyde Thomas wanted to ask the Angel of Childhood Dreams why he was dressed as a mail carrier, but he thought it would be rude. Instead, he answered, "I didn't know I could see magic in the mirror."

"My good boy, of course you can! Haven't you looked into it yet?" Ralph asked.

"Well, I did look into the mirror when I found it. But I didn't see anything magical. I only saw myself," Clyde Thomas replied.

"Did you like what you saw?" asked Ralph, settling down comfortably on his bulging mailbag.

"I guess so." Clyde Thomas felt a little confused and tried to assure himself that this was only a dream.

"If you could see something different," Ralph continued, "what would you see?"

"Well," answered Clyde Thomas slowly, "I'd like to be a little taller. I'm growing slowly but I still feel short. Sometimes, at school, the other kids call me Shrimp Boy."

Smiling, Ralph asked, "What is it that tall boys do that you don't do?"

"Oh, you know," Clyde Thomas mumbled, head hung low, "they stand up straight. They puff out their chests. They look the soccer coach right in the eye. They are not shy!" he finished, tilting his head to peer at Ralph.

"Oh, that's all, is it!" Ralph laughed and slapped the side of the mailbag, causing several letters to spill on the floor. "Then, do this, boy," he said. "Look into the mirror and say, 'I am a tall boy. Even if I only measure four feet on the scale at school, I am still a very tall boy.'"

This seemed like silly talk to Clyde Thomas, but since it was only a dream, and he didn't expect to wake up very soon, he gave it a try. Looking deeply into the mirror, staring at his own face, he slowly repeated Ralph's words.

"I am a tall boy. Even if I only measure four feet on the scale at school, I am still a very tall boy." Suddenly Clyde Thomas felt himself straighten up. Standing erect, he held his head high with a strength he didn't feel before. In the mirror, Clyde Thomas really did look taller.

Nodding and smiling, Ralph said, "See yourself as a tall boy, and the world will see a tall boy!" The very next moment Ralph disappeared, and Clyde Thomas felt the morning sun streaming across his cheeks.

Sitting down at the breakfast table, shoulders straight and head held high, Clyde Thomas called to his mother, "I am taller today,

Mother! See how tall I am!"

"Why, yes, Clyde Thomas," his mother answered, turning from her cooking to look at him. "You do look taller today! Goodness! My, how you children are growin'!"

All day long, Clyde Thomas smiled as if he had some secret. He sat up very straight in his chair at school so that everyone could see how tall he felt. When it came time for the school boys to be divided into teams for soccer, Clyde Thomas stood up tall as a tree and puffed out his chest.

Scratching his head, the coach said, "I don't know how I missed you last week, Clyde Thomas. I should have put you on a different team. You are bigger than I remembered!"

All day long Clyde Thomas felt so tall, he acted taller. Everyone he met looked at him differently, as if seeing him for the first time.

That night, just before bed, he quietly took the mirror out from under his clothes in the drawer and looked into it. "Sure enough!" he smiled at himself. "The ocean gave me a very special gift. Tonight," he said, peering into the mirror, "I'll become smarter!"

Tucking the mirror back under his clothes, he climbed into bed and fell asleep. Right on schedule, Ralph, dressed in his postal uniform, traveled into the dreams of Clyde Thomas.

"Say, fellow! You, there, Tall Boy!" he called. "I hear you're looking into the mirror to be smarter!"

"Yes, sir!" answered Clyde Thomas. "You should have seen me at school today! Man, was I tall! Now, I want to be smart, too!"

"Well, what is it that smart boys do?" asked Ralph, sitting on the floor and leaning on his mailbag.

"They look right at the teacher and answer questions. And even if they get the questions wrong, they don't worry, because they are smart. They know they will read the right answers in a book later!" Clyde Thomas replied.

"Do they read a lot?" asked Ralph.

"You know they do!" answered Clyde Thomas. "They do because they are smart. It all goes with being smart!"

"So," said Ralph, punching his mailbag into a more comfortable shape, "look into the mirror and say, 'I am a smart boy. I read all the time because I am such a smarty! My grades get better and better because I am so smart, and because I read so much!'" This time Clyde Thomas didn't think the angel was fooling. He looked into the mirror and repeated each word exactly.

"I am a smart boy. I read all the time because I am such a smarty! My grades get better and better because I am so smart, and because I read so much!"

"See yourself as a smart boy," said Ralph, "and the world will see a smart boy!" Laughing a hearty laugh, the angel melted into his mailbag, which then melted into nothingness. The very next instant, Clyde Thomas woke to the smell of bacon frying in a pan as his mother prepared breakfast.

"Here comes Clyde Thomas!" his mother said, surprised, "and he's readin' a book!" Walking to the breakfast table, Clyde Thomas kept his nose buried deep in a history book.

"Don't bother me now, Mother. I'm reading. I have some questions to answer in school today!" Continuing to read, Clyde Thomas ate breakfast with one hand and held his book with the other.

"I don't know what's happenin' to that boy," his mother said to Uncle Frazier. Shaking her head as she pushed scrambled eggs onto a plate, she continued, "just yesterday, I could swear he'd gotten taller. And now, well, our young man seems to be gettin' smarter too!" Grinning behind his book, Clyde Thomas kept his secret to himself.

Reading all the way to school, Clyde Thomas knew all about the history lesson when he got to class. Raising his hand for almost every question, he surprised his teacher.

"What's gotten into you, Clyde Thomas?" she asked after class. "Are you getting smarter, or what?" Clyde Thomas only smiled, keeping his secret quiet.

After school he played soccer with his friends, running fast, the way tall boys do, and out-guessing the other team, the way the smart boys do. Late that afternoon a very happy Clyde Thomas ran down the beach toward his house.

On the way home he saw the new girl, just a year behind him in school, sitting beside the ocean, crying. Feeling smart, he ran right over to her.

"Hi!" he said, smiling cheerfully.

Turning her head in the other direction and looking down at the ground, the girl cried softly.

"Hey, what's the matter, girl?" Clyde Thomas asked, dropping down to sit on the sand next to her.

"Oh. Oh," she blushed and stuttered. "Oh, nothing." She hung her head even lower.

What would a smart boy do in a situation like this? Clyde Thomas wondered. 'I guess he'd try to figure out what was the matter by acting like the girl.' Slumping down, Clyde Thomas sniffled softly and looked away from her. As he did so, she glanced over at him through her long, dark lashes. Feeling the girl look at him, Clyde Thomas began to feel shy and a little bit afraid. 'That must be it,' he thought to himself, 'I bet she's feeling shy because she's new to this island!'

Sitting quietly, Clyde Thomas tried to decide what to say or do. Just then, the girl whispered softly, "I'm surprised to see you here. You are that tall, smart boy from the grade ahead of mine. Why are you sitting here with me?"

"Because," Clyde Thomas answered, "you are new to this island,

23

and I bet you're lonesome. I want to help. I want
to be your friend."

At his words, the girl sat up. Drying her eyes
with the back of her hand, she smiled shyly at Clyde
Thomas. "You really are smart!" she said. "I do feel
lonesome. I've been here a whole week and nobody,
that is until you, has talked to me at school. I'm really
shy and it's hard for me to make friends. That's why I'm
crying. How did you know?"

"Lucky guess!" smiled Clyde Thomas, leaning back
on his elbows next to the girl. "Well, now, if you could be
anything you wanted to be," he said, using the words of
the mail carrying angel, "what would it be?"

"I'd like to be popular! I'd like to be outgoing and not
so shy!"

"Well, then," Clyde Thomas went on, starting to feel almost like
an angel himself, "what is it that popular kids do, that you don't do?"

"Oh, that's easy," said the girl excitedly. "They look right at
everybody, they smile, and they walk up to new kids and say, 'Hi, my
name is so and so and I'm new here. What a pretty dress you have on
today! What is your name?' " She laughed at herself as she imitated the
popular kids from her old school.

Looking at Clyde Thomas, she waited for what he would do next.
He was stumped. Confused, he reviewed the problem in his mind. If
she was going to get over her shyness and become popular, she would
have to use the magic mirror. But, if he gave her the mirror, he would
be giving away his gift from the ocean. The gift would be hers, and he
would no longer have the magic. Suddenly, he panicked. He really
didn't want to give away the magic mirror, his gift from the ocean. He
liked being smart. He liked being tall.

"Well," he said abruptly, "I'm sorry you're so shy. You really are
pretty; you probably could have some friends if you tried. I have to go

now." Without even asking her name, he stood up and began to sprint away down the beach toward his home. Running from the girl, Clyde Thomas felt awful inside. He didn't have to turn his head to know she would be slumped over, crying again.

"Ah, shoot!" he said to himself. Turning around, he headed back up the beach to the girl. He was right. She was sitting there, crying. This time she didn't look at him at all.

"I'm sorry," he said, "I wasn't being very nice. Listen, don't cry. I have a secret. I know how you can be popular. I just didn't want to give away my secret. That's why I left. Please don't cry."

Sniffing, the girl looked up at Clyde Thomas. "You will help me?"

"Yes," he smiled, holding out his hand for her to take. "Come with me to my family's home, and I'll share my secret with you. C'mon," he said, pulling her up. "Let's run! It's only a short way!"

Running down the beach, the two children laughed, chased seagulls, and raced along the sand. Once at his home, Clyde Thomas asked the girl to sit on the porch and wait for him. He went to his room and pulled the magic mirror out from under his clothes in the drawer. Looking into the mirror, he gave a long sigh. Tucking it into his back pocket, he went outside and sat on the porch next to her.

"Now," he said, "I'm going to give you something magical. It's very special and you must keep it a secret, okay?" Solemnly, the girl nodded yes. Pulling the mirror out from his pocket he handed it to her.

"It's just a little plastic mirror," she said, wondering if Clyde Thomas really was as smart as everyone seemed to think.

"No, it's a magical mirror," he insisted. "Now, look in the mirror and repeat after me. 'I am a popular girl. Everybody likes me. I walk right up to people and say 'Hello!' I smile at people and look them in the eyes. I am a popular girl!'" Thinking that Clyde Thomas was acting very strangely, the girl decided it would be best to do what he said, and then to go directly home. Carefully she turned the mirror over and peered into it. Gazing into her own eyes, she slowly repeated Clyde

Thomas' words.

"I am a popular girl. Everybody likes me. I walk right up to people and say "Hello!" I smile at people and look them in the eyes. I am a popular girl!" As she finished, she began sitting just a little bit straighter. Looking up at Clyde Thomas, amazed, she stuttered, "I... I feel better! I... I feel..." searching for a word, she hesitated.

"You feel popular!" Clyde Thomas finished her sentence.

"Yes!" she wondered in amazement.

"That's the magic of the mirror," Clyde Thomas explained. "You see yourself as a popular girl, and the world will see you as a popular girl!"

Just then, Uncle Frazier rounded the corner of the house. "Well, now, boy. Who dis' new girl?" he asked.

"This is my friend..." stopping in mid-sentence, Clyde Thomas realized he didn't know her name. He'd given away his magic mirror, and he didn't even know the girl's name!

"Antoinette!" the girl finished his sentence. "Hello!" Standing up and looking directly into Uncle Frazier's eyes, Antoinette smiled a big, shining smile.

"Well, hello!" Uncle Frazier smiled back. "I be Frazier, da Rasta mon. So pleased to be meetin' you, girl! Hope ta be seein' you 'round more! Maybe you can be a stayin' for dinner?" Winking at Clyde Thomas, Uncle Frazier sauntered into the house, dredlocks swaying back and forth as he walked.

"Oh! Dinner!" Antoinette jumped up from the porch steps. "It must be time for me to get home! Mother will be worried!" Looking at Clyde Thomas and smiling happily, she blushed. "Thank you so much for this wonderful gift, Clyde Thomas. You are my first friend on this island, and you are very special! See you in school!" Slipping the magic mirror into the pocket of her dress and bounding down the steps, she waved and skipped out of the yard and back down the beach toward her home.

Sinking inside, Clyde Thomas slumped over. Suddenly he didn't feel like sitting up straight. He didn't feel like reading. He felt awful. "I gave the magic away!" he thought miserably. Slowly he got up and shuffled into the house.

"Time for dinner, son!" his mother called from the kitchen. "Uncle Frazier says you've got a real pretty new friend. Come tell me about her while you wash up!"

"I don't feel hungry, Mother," mumbled Clyde Thomas, hanging his head and shuffling toward his room. "I'm just going to bed."

"Now, what ever's got' into that boy?" wondered his mother aloud to Uncle Frazier as they set the dinner table.

Feeling absolutely terrible, Clyde Thomas climbed into bed, pulled the sheet over his head, hiding from his family and from everything. Trying hard to forget the magic mirror, he closed his eyes and, finally, fell asleep.

In the middle of the night, the thud of a heavy mail bag dropping on the floor of his room woke Clyde Thomas with a start.

"Hey, it's you! Shouldn't you be with Antoinette now? I mean, she's the one with the magic mirror, not me!" Clyde Thomas said bitterly, noticing Ralph at the foot of his bed.

"Now, boy!" said Ralph cheerfully. "I can't imagine a smart boy talking so foolish! What's the problem here?"

"Well," said Clyde Thomas, "it's just that I gave the magic mirror away to that new girl, Antoinette. She seemed so sad and lonely, and I knew the magic would make her popular. And, from the way she greeted Uncle Frazier, I'd say it started working right off!"

"So, boy, what's the problem?" Ralph asked, arranging his mailbag into a cushy chair. "Sounds to me like you did the right thing! You should be happy over that!"

"Well, now she has the magic, and I don't. I'll go back to being short and not so smart. That's the problem!" Frowning, Clyde Thomas crossed his arms in front of his chest. Sighing heavily, he slumped down.

"Oh, ho! What a silly boy!" laughed Ralph.

"Why are you laughing at me?" scowled Clyde Thomas.

"Don't you know, boy? The magic isn't in the mirror! The magic is in your eyes! You just use the mirror to look into your magic eyes. That's all! The magic happens when you see yourself the way you want the world to see you. The mirror just reflects who you really are inside. You can look into any mirror, or any shiny plate, or even into a smooth puddle of water! The magic is in your eyes, my boy!"

"Really?" asked Clyde Thomas, sitting up.

"Yes, of course," Ralph nodded, "and, I'd say, not only are you a tall boy, and a smart boy, but anyone as generous and as helpful as you are must be a pretty special boy as well!"

"Gee, I never thought of it that way!" Clyde Thomas broke into a smile. "Thanks, Ralph!"

"No problem, my boy! Well, I've got several stops to make tonight. Better get going."

"Ralph," asked Clyde Thomas, "before you go, can you tell me why an angel is dressed like a postal carrier? And what's in all those letters you deliver?"

"Sure thing, boy." Grinning, Ralph slung the bag over one shoulder. "These are the dreams, hopes and wishes of children. When a child sends a dream into the universe, I deliver it! The more clear the address, that is, the more clearly the child knows what he or she wants, the easier it is for me to make the delivery! Simple system, really. Now, I'm off. Remember," he said smiling at Clyde Thomas, "the real magic is always inside of you. Just look into your own eyes and know who you are! Bye, boy!"

As Ralph disappeared into the night, Clyde Thomas lay back on his bed and smiled. Before falling asleep, he stretched one big, long stretch. It was the kind of stretch that tall boys make.

"Bravo! Good job! Great story, Stanley!" Raising his claws to clap for the storytelling sand crab, Fool found them replaced by his own hands, firmly attached to his own arms. "What?" he exclaimed loudly. Shaking himself from his dream, Fool sat up, looked around, and felt himself safe and sound in the warm, now very dark, cave. His friends, Intuit and the old brown bear, snored away contentedly.

"Ah... oh... just dreaming," he muttered to himself settling back down into a comfortable position. Reaching over, he wrapped his arm around the sleeping dog, and soon joined his friends in a chorus of snores.

In his sleep, Intuit felt the love in Fool's hug. Wriggling with happiness, the little dog remembered the boat ride he'd shared with Fool in the early summer. Rocking softly in a boat filled with memories, Intuit rode a gentle wave of love directly into a doggy dream. This is the story Intuit dreamed while sleeping soundly in the cave with Fool and the old brown bear.

Intuit's Dream

Where Intuit dreams of a fisherman, a pelican and
a famous sailing dog.

"Well, maties, that's the way I know it to be. Yes, sirs, that's the way this old salt heard the tale." Untangling another knot from his fishing net, Captain Scalewell winked at his audience.

"Tell us another, Captain Scalewell! Tell us another story!" Clapping their hands, five ragged children sitting in a circle around the old fisherman begged for another sea story. Two bone thin dogs lying in the warm afternoon sun slapped their tails on the wooden dock in agreement. A big pelican, perched high on top of a piling, stretched his rubbery blue neck. Then, spreading his enormous wings, he fanned the air and nodded.

"Yes, another story!" the huge bird seemed to say.

Leaning back against the wall of his fishing shanty, Captain Scalewell set his net aside for a moment and began filling his big, clay pipe. Knowing that a new bowlful of sweet smelling cherry tobacco most certainly meant another story, the children grew quiet.

Taking his time, Captain Scalewell tapped tobacco into the bowl of his pipe. The old man's face, creased with deep wrinkles, was tanned dark from the sun. His scruffy, gray-speckled beard matched the weather-worn fishing dock. Bushy

30

brows stuck out forming little awnings over his eyes. He wore a faded red and white shirt under a patch-covered navy blue jacket. His pants were stained with boat engine oil and his once bright yellow rain boots were dirty and scuffed. He didn't sail, or even fish very often anymore, mostly because arthritis had caused his fingers to curl up into knots much like the ones that tangled his fishing nets. Instead, he sat outside his little shanty next to the pier, breathed in salty sea air, mended nets and wove sea yarns for the children who lived in the fishing village nearby.

The children, who listened so raptly to his stories, wore old, ragged clothing and went barefoot because their parents were too poor to buy shoes. Sea breezes tossed stringy hair around thin faces. Faces that almost always, despite their poverty, smiled brightly.

Lighting his pipe and drawing in a big hiss of air, Captain Scalewell let out a thick cloud of cherry-scented smoke. "Well, just one more. Then it's off with the lot of you. I'm a busy fisherman. Does it look like I have time to sit around talking to a bunch of scally-waggle kids and their mangy mutts everyday?" Pretending to be gruff, he settled into his chair and began his favorite activity, storytelling.

"Speaking of mutts," he began, looking at one of the dogs listlessly scratching fleas, "here's a story about a sailing dog, a famous sailing dog, at that." Leaning toward the children, the old fisherman began his tale.

31

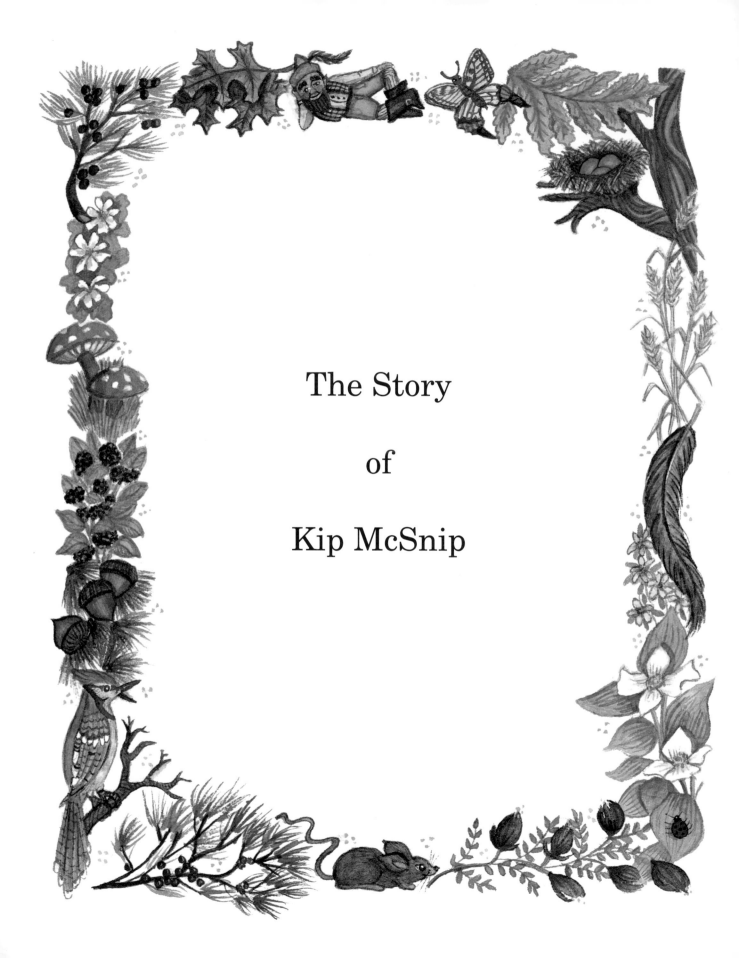

The Story

of

Kip McSnip

Chapter Two

The Story of Kip McSnip

Kip McSnip was a salty dog.
And he sailed the seas of the world,
With a keen-eyed captain, a Siamese cat
and a lovely, red-haired girl.

Adapted from, The Ballad of
Kip MacSnip by George O. Allaman, III

His name was Kip McSnip, The Sailing Dog. Kip McSnip lived on a small boat named *Reve* which means "Dream" in French. Folks used to say the boat was as pretty as a little dream. Painted bright white with a tomato red stripe around her bow, she bobbed pleasantly in the water when the winds were calm. When the winds blew briskly, her red and white-striped sails filled round and full, and she skipped over the waves like a flying fish skimming over lively summer seas. Sailing *Reve* with confidence, her skipper, Captain George, hoisted the jib, pulled in the lines, and reefed the mainsail all like the experienced sailor he was. Captain George's strong arms rippled with muscles as he worked, and his face wore a smile that was wide and ready. Folks say his eyes were as blue as the sea itself.

Captain George sailed in the company of a beautiful red-haired girl, a Siamese cat, and, of course, the sailing dog, Kip McSnip. The red-haired girl was known from one side of the ocean to the other for her beauty, and for the way she danced. Shining in the hot sun, her hair looked like a hundred brand new pennies spilling to the ground. At night, under a billion silver stars, she danced on the bow of *Reve*. Her emerald green eyes snapped and sparkled, and the gold rings in her ears, and even the one she wore on her toe, flashed and glittered as she leapt and twirled with the music. When Captain George took out his guitar to play her a song, all the mermaids, dolphins, whales and other creatures of the sea came to the surface to watch the red-haired girl twirl and dip to the music of the captain's tunes. Seagulls swept from the skies to sit along *Reve's* lifelines, reserving front row seats for the dance performance. At the end of the dance, those noisy gulls cawed and flapped their wings, beating the air! The whales blew towering streams of water from their blow holes, the mermaids cheered and clapped wildly, while the dolphins slapped the water with their tails. What a noisy audience!

The Siamese cat was lazy and fat. During the day, he slept on the soft cushions in the cabin of the boat. When Kip McSnip or Captain George walked by, he'd simply open one eye, just a slit, heave a sigh and drift back to sleep, ignoring them with disdain. If the red-haired girl walked past, she'd bend down and pet him a time or two, and the lazy old cat would purr contentedly in his sleep. At night, he patrolled the boat, searching every line and every board for stray ship mice or little brown cockroaches.

Now, Kip McSnip! What a very special dog he was! His fluffy fur grew in all different directions as if three large cows had licked it into place when he was a puppy. He looked like a patchwork quilt of brown, white and black. One pale, sky blue eye, and one deep hazel eye with flecks of gold added to his comical appearance. His tail looked like a feather duster waving back and forth all the time, except when he was sleeping. That dog loved to swim, he did. Jumping over the side of *Reve* every morning for his daily swim in the calm, blue ocean, he chased large green turtles through waves the way land-locked dogs chase cars down country roads. Tiring of turtle chasing, he'd climb *Reve's* boarding ladder, shake sea water in a fine, wide spray, and settle in the sunlight for a doggy daydream or two. Whenever the red-haired girl danced on the bow of the boat, Kip McSnip joined in, jumping and barking loudly.

Little *Reve* and her crew made a joyful, happy show. *Reve*, floating under the moonlight, the Siamese cat on cockroach patrol, handsome Captain George strumming a Spanish song on his guitar, the red-haired girl leaping and dancing to the music, and Kip McSnip prancing and barking in accompaniment. A host of sea creatures swaying and clapping in time with the music added to the party.

Reve sailed over many seas with Kip McSnip standing at her bow, barking at dolphins leaping merrily along side as the small boat slid through deep, blue waves.

All was fine for many, many months. Then, one day, the clouds turned from fluffy, puffy white, to a dark, heavy gray. The seas turned from bright, sparkling blue to a velvet indigo, the color of ink in a bottle. The warm, sun-kissed breeze turned to a sharp, icy cold wind blowing the sails of *Reve* in different directions. The once calm ocean became a roaring sea monster, rising up high into the air with *Reve* perched uneasily on its back. SLAM! The sea monster crashed back into the ocean. SPLAT! *Reve* smacked hard against the surface of the rough sea. Then back up again, the monster reared, snarling and spewing spouts of frothy white foam. CRASH! Down into the sea it hurled the little boat again.

"Oh! Oh! Help!" cried the red-haired girl, her long skirts swirling around her legs in the wind. "*Reve* will be smashed to bits!"

"Don't worry! I can handle her!" called Captain George. But despite his strength, and his bravery, the angry sea was a much stronger and fiercer opponent than the captain had imagined. Scurrying for cover, the Siamese cat huddled below decks under a pile of maps and charts.

Kip McSnip barked and growled and howled and bared his teeth at the huge waves. Towering high in the shape of giant dragons, the waves curled and crashed down over the frightened boat and crew. Rising up and down, up and down, in the fury of the ocean, *Reve* shuddered, her very planks shaking.

"We're doomed!" shouted the captain to the red-haired girl as a giant gust of wind ripped the mainsail into two, large ragged pieces. "Grab McSnip and go below! There's nothing we can do now, except pray!"

At the same time, Kip McSnip was having ideas of his own. "I won't let my best friends, and my favorite little boat, be hurt this way!" he thought. "There must be something I can do... I'm going for help!" Escaping the red-haired girl's grasp, McSnip hurled himself over the side of the bounding boat, deep, deep into the frothy, foamy water.

Poor Kip McSnip! Despite kicking out his legs as fast as he could go, the huge and fierce waves lifted him high into the air, and tossed the little dog about like a volleyball. Suddenly a giant wave grabbed him from the air, wrapped its foamy arms around him and pulled him far, far under the sea. Holding his breath the very best he could, and squeezing his eyes shut tightly, McSnip felt himself plummeting deeper and deeper below the surface of the ocean. Underwater so long that he seemed to be falling asleep, he began to imagine he was drifting rather than crashing through the water. Down, down, down he went. Past flickering mermaid lamps deep below the surface. Down, down, down, past silent ghost ships leaning on their sides on the coral-covered sea bed. Then, suddenly, McSnip felt a pulling upward, and he began to spin round and round, and up and up until a giant hand seemed to toss him right out of the water, high into the air.

"Poooh!" Kip McSnip let out the stale air with a whoosh. Fresh, cold air rushed in, filling his gasping lungs. Then splash! Falling back into the sea, and treading water in the swirling, churning waves, McSnip began to think that he was going to drown before he could ever reach shore. But, instead of crying or panicking, the little dog got mad. Madder than he'd ever been before.

"Bark! Bark! Growl! Snarl! Bark!" He began to make more noise than any dog had ever made! "You can drown me, you nasty old ocean!" he barked wildly, "but not without a fight!" Paddling around furiously and barking at the top of his lungs, spitting water, ducking under, then paddling to the surface again, McSnip waged a one dog war with the ocean.

Suddenly, a giant flash of lightning lit the sky, and a thunder clap split the ocean in two. Rising up from the bottom of the sea came a

37

huge, glistening, jet black coral trident. Holding the trident, was the muscled arm of the very King of the Sea... King Neptune himself!

King Neptune loomed as tall as a mountain. His crown, made of fire coral flaming orange, red and yellow, matched the radiance of his sparkling black eyes, while his beard, like millions of tangled sea snails, curled in a hundred different directions.

"Lo!" he thundered, rising from the watery depths. "Who is making all this noise during my perfect storm? Who is disturbing my game? Who challenges the King of the Sea?"

In the presence of their great king, the waves parted respectfully and hung back, suspended in time. McSnip paddled in circles, straining his neck as he stared up at the gigantic sea king.

"It's me, sir, your royal highness, sir," barked McSnip. "I want the sea to stop hurting my friends aboard the boat, *Reve*. I love them with all my heart, and I'll do anything to save them!"

"What? Well, who are you, you half-drowned creature?" Bending over, King Neptune reached down and placed his hand flat on the water. Scrambling onto this giant platform, Kip held his breath as he rose skyward on the king's hand. Holding McSnip at eye level, the great king stared at the shivering dog. In King Neptune's palm, McSnip looked about the same size as a tiny toy turtle in the hands of a small child. "Well, little fellow," said the king more gently, "why should I stop a perfectly good storm just for you? What can you offer me?"

Thinking hard, McSnip thought of what he did best. "I can guard for you! I'm a wonderful guard dog, and I can bark louder and more furiously than any dog on earth!"

"Ho, ho!" laughed the giant king, "I can agree with that for sure! You barked so loudly you brought me up from the bottom of the ocean!"

"Well, then," McSnip hurried on, "let me guard your palace below the waves. I'll guard your seas day and night. I'll bark at all who try to harm your pets and your friends, the whales, the dolphins, the turtles, and even those pesky gulls. And," he added, "when fishermen catch dolphins, I'll swim over and chew through those awful nets. I'll let the dolphins go free! But, please, let the little boat *Reve* and her crew live. Stop this storm so they can sail away safely!"

"Hmm," said the king, stroking his curly beard with one hand, "you mean to say that you'd trade your life to save the ones you love?"

"Yes, King Neptune, I'll do anything to save my captain, the red-haired girl, and that lazy old cat!"

"Well," mused the giant, "you wouldn't last an hour in my ocean kingdom. Besides, my sea lions make powerful guards. But I respect your courage, little dog, and your willingness to give yourself for those you love. And, maybe, with all that barking, there is something you can do to help me."

"Anything! Just say the word, King!" barked McSnip.

"You know," said Neptune, "on the land there are many, many plastic things. Things that hold soda pop and beer cans together. Plastic bottles, plastic pens, plastic razors, and even plastic toys."

"Yes, of course," said McSnip, thinking about all the plastic items aboard *Reve*.

"Well, sometimes people get careless and toss plastic things into the sea," Neptune continued. "Even when they are thrown into garbage pails some of them end up finding their way to the ocean. My little seals, dolphins, whales, and turtles think they are food, or pretty necklaces. When sea creatures swallow or get tangled in plastic, they die."

"Oh, no!" gasped McSnip, remembering the beautiful dolphins as they jumped and raced along next to *Reve*.

"It's true," said King Neptune, solemnly. "I love my little sea creatures just as much as you love the captain, and the rest of the crew. It makes me very sad and very, very angry when my loved ones suffer. Stay on that little boat of yours, Kip McSnip. Sail everywhere in the world and tell everyone you meet to recycle their plastic things. And tell them, especially, to never, never throw anything plastic into the water!

Bark loudly at everyone you see using plastic of any kind. Remind them of my wonderful sea creatures, and help to keep them alive and happy." Looking straight into Kip McSnip's eyes, the great King asked, "Will you do that, little dog?"

"Oh, yes, King Neptune!" answered Kip McSnip. "I'll bark your message around the world until everyone hears it!"

"Well, then, my little friend," smiled the king, "go home to your friends!"

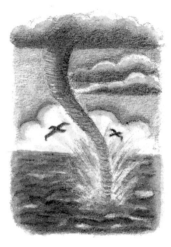

Setting McSnip gently in the water, the great king grabbed his trident with both hands and began churning the ocean as if he were stirring a pot of stew with a giant, wooden spoon.

Round and round the ocean swirled, creating a huge water spout. The spout sucked McSnip up, up and away, and carried him whirling across the ocean right up to the little boat, *Reve*. Twisting by the boat, the water spout tossed McSnip onto the deck.

"Oh, McSnip! You're alive! We thought you were gone forever!" called the red-haired girl, rushing over to hug the soaking little dog.

"McSnip, you're just in time!" exclaimed Captain George. "The storm seems to be settling down! We're going to turn on the motor and head for land to get our sails repaired. Don't go off for a swim during storms, ever again! We need you here on the boat!"

McSnip grinned a big, doggy grin at his friends and plopped down on the deck to sleep. He was a very, very tired little dog! As he slept, the ocean calmed completely, and a beautiful sun rose high and swept gracefully across the sky. Captain George spent a relaxing day repairing damage to the boat, the red-haired girl practiced her dance steps on the bow of *Reve*, and the old, fat cat spent hours licking salt water off McSnip's matted fur.

"And that's the story of Kip McSnip, the sailing dog," Captain Scalewell said, taking his now cold pipe from his mouth.

"But did he tell people about the plastic?" a shy, wide-eyed little girl spoke up.

"Oh, yes, that!" Captain Scalewell winked. "Almost forgot that part. Kip McSnip did try to tell people, mostly grownups. But many of them were too busy to listen. So he began to bark to other dogs, and even to a few cats. He told them about the plastics and about what plastics do to sea animals. Soon, dogs and cats all around the world began to tell children about plastic. Because, as you know," the Captain said, looking straight at the little girl who had asked the question, "animals and children seem to be able to understand each other." Slap, slap, slap went the tail of one of the skinny dogs on the pier. Smiling, the little girl reached over and petted the dog's head. Flap, flap, flap, went the giant wings of the old, blue-necked pelican, for he, too, understood.

"Anyway," the captain went on, "McSnip told the animals of the world, and they told the children of the world about plastic. He told them how to cut the round things that hold cans together, and he told them how to recycle bottles and other things. The children began to recycle plastic, and they helped their parents shop for containers that could be recycled."

"Did the ocean become safe for the sea creatures?" asked a thin, freckled boy sitting on a pile of nets.

"Sort of," answered the fisherman. "You see, cleaning up the ocean isn't something you can just do once and be done. Keeping the earth and her waters clean is a part of life, today and forever. That's why," said Captain Scalewell, winking at the boy, "Kip McSnip is still out there, on a little white boat, barking his message to all the animals and children of the world!" Knocking ashes from his pipe, he went on, "next time you see a dog barking on a boat, wave and say 'Hi!' He could just be the famous sailing dog, Kip McSnip!"

Deeply asleep, Intuit heard the barking of Kip McSnip floating on the wind. Dreaming of running to shore to greet the sailing dog, he pawed the air and wagged his tail. All his wiggling woke the old bear.

"Hurrumph!" mumbled the bear, moving out of range of Intuit's racing paws. "That silly creature must be chasing squirrels in his sleep!" Groaning and yawning, the bear settled down again. Within moments he drifted into a dream of his own.

The Old Brown Bear's Dream

<u>Where the bear becomes a cub again,
and visits a gypsy camp.</u>

The old brown bear had a hard time recalling much of anything these days. But sometimes, just before he slipped into sleep, he remembered being a bear cub. In those days he lived with his mother and a band of roving gypsies. Traveling all over the land, the gypsies stopped in towns and villages to put on fairs, shows and circuses. It was pleasant to drift into sleep thinking of those special times. As he slid between awake and asleep, he saw the gypsy camp, every detail pictured clearly in his mind. At the sight of the camp, the old bear smiled to himself and tumbled into very deep sleep. For a while, the old bear became a cub again, and looking around, he observed the gypsy camp through the eyes of a baby bear.

Each gypsy family had its own brightly colored wagon pulled by a team of dancing black and white horses. Wearing wavy fluffy feathers and shiny brass bells on their harnesses, the horses pranced in formation, causing the bells to tinkle loudly and the feathers to fan the air.

Wherever the gypsies stopped and set up camp, the countryside changed from tranquil farm life to a kaleidoscope of color, music and laughter. Hundreds of tents, looking like piles of dazzling birthday gifts, sprang up as if by magic. Flags fluttered and slapped in the winds that whirled through the gypsy camp. Handsome gypsy men strutted past the tents and wagons in tight black pants, tall leather boots, and flowing red satin shirts. Olive-skinned women with dark, snapping eyes tossed manes of long, black hair and twirled around in brilliantly colored silky skirts.

The bear cub loved traveling with the gypsies. Such adventure! Such excitement!

Looking cute was the only responsibility of the bear cub, and he did his job without even thinking. Mother bear performed in the center ring of the gypsy circus. Featured as **The World's Most Wild Bear,** her job demanded a great deal of acting skill. While audiences shuddered and drew back in fear, mother bear roared and slashed the air with her mighty paws. Cracking his leather whip with a SNAP! and lifting a red and gold stool high in the air, the brave trainer held mother bear back from the crowds. Mother bear acted as fierce as possible while the trainer acted as brave as any man could. The braver the trainer appeared, and the more ferocious mother bear seemed, the more the crowds clapped and cheered. And, the more they encouraged their friends and neighbors to go and see **The World's Most Wild Bear.**

The bear cub, the trainer and all the gypsies knew the entire show was simply pretend. But gypsies are very good at letting people believe whatever they most wish, and so, the crowds went home talking about the fierceness of bears, and the braveness, or foolishness, of gypsy bear trainers.

Each night after the show when all the townspeople left, the trainer sat on the red and gold stool inside the bear cage, feeding grapes to mother bear and her cub. Holding a small bunch of fruit between his fingers, the bear trainer whispered gentle words of praise and appreciation to mother bear for her performance that day. Using the tip of her long, pink tongue, mother bear delicately, being ever so lady-like, plucked single grapes from the bunch, slowly savoring their sweet flavor.

Most of all, the bear cub enjoyed gazing through the bars of his cage to the half open tent of Madam Bonita, the Fortune Teller. People from towns and villages visiting the gypsy camp often passed Madam Bonita's booth saying things like, "Oh that's just fake! No one believes in fortune tellers! She just makes that stuff up!" But the bear cub noticed many people sneaking back later to hear about their futures, their loves and their fortunes.

Townspeople and villagers weren't the only ones to visit Madam Bonita. Gypsies often visited her as well. But Madam Bonita never took money from other gypsies for telling their fortunes, and the gypsies were not embarrassed to be seen asking her questions.

Falling deeper and deeper into sleep, the bear began to relive his favorite dream of gypsies and their noisy, brightly colored camp. This is the old bear's dream about Shena, a little gypsy girl, and her special miracle.

Shena's Miracle

Chapter Three

Shena's Miracle

Madam Bonita's long, thin fingers stroked the smooth, round crystal ball. A purple satin handkerchief held down the fortune teller's wild, curly, black hair. Her earrings were huge hoops of silver. Rings sparkled on every finger, each one holding a beautiful shiny stone, or a carving in gold, pearl or jet black onyx. Layers of multi-colored beads and silver necklaces circled her neck. Silver bracelets covering her arms jingled whenever she moved.

Sitting quietly next to the gypsy woman, Shena, a young gypsy girl, listened and watched. Fascinated with the fortune teller's craft, Shena hoped that someday she would be able to read advice from the crystal ball, the gypsy cards, the tea leaves, and the palms of customers.

"I see. Yes, I see," said Madam Bonita, pausing a moment to look at the young man sitting in front of her.

Leaning forward, her client asked, "What, what do you see, gypsy woman?" Squinting his eyes, he tried peering into the crystal ball.

"I see flowers. Yellow flowers with maybe, yes...."

"With what?" Leaning over the ball, the man almost bumped into Madam Bonita's head.

"With, maybe, some red. Yes, some red. And I see you, with the flowers in your hand." Madam Bonita looked up from the ball. "Do you have a pretty young lady in your thoughts right now?" she asked him gently.

"Oh, oh, you must be seeing Susan! She's the most beautiful girl in the whole village! How did you know?"

"Madam Bonita knows many things." Smiling, the gypsy stroked the ball again. "There seems to be someone else here," she continued. "Another young man, I think."

"That's Jack! I knew it! He's got his eyes on Susan! He's just a bully and would never take care of her," he said, shaking his head back and forth.

Shena looked up at Madam Bonita and whispered, "Can you help him to win the heart of Susan?"

Madam Bonita winked at Shena, ever so slightly. Gazing deep into the crystal globe, she went on. "I see a great cloud of dust. Maybe a fight between two men. You must be careful, young man. Strength will not win this battle. Cunning, and wit, will win this fight. You must be very careful, and you must be very clever," Madam Bonita warned. "But, I do see your hand on the flowers, and I see the hand of a young woman on the flowers, too." Taking her hands off the ball Madam Bonita brushed them across her forehead. "It's gone blurry, that's all I can see for now."

"Oh, you've been a great help!" said the young man digging into his pockets to find coins to pay the fortune teller. "It's that Jack, and he's going to try and fight for Susan. But I won't fight! I'll figure a way to outsmart him! Then I'll give Susan flowers, and she'll love me. Oh, thank you! Thank you! Now I know how to win Susan's heart!"

Pressing coins into the gypsy woman's hand, the young man thanked her once more and hurried off to look for red and yellow flowers. Madam Bonita slipped her hand into the folds of her flowing crimson skirt, and the coins disappeared.

Turning to Shena, Madam Bonita asked, "And you, my little one, what would you like to hear today?"

Shena blushed and giggled a little, then slapped her hand over her mouth. Growing in at different angles, her two front teeth had separated leaving a gap between them. Embarrassed by the gap, Shena tried hard to avoid smiling in front of people.

"Oh, sweetheart, don't worry about that little gap, it's just part of you right now. You are a wonderful little girl!" Reaching over, the gypsy woman gave Shena a quick hug. Smiling for just a second, Shena quickly put her hand over her mouth again.

"Let's turn a card or two and see what's in store for our little Shena, shall we?" Picking up her well-worn deck, Madam Bonita shuffled, then pulled out two cards. One by one she laid them face down on the table. Slowly, she turned over the first card. It showed a large, stone tower next to a dark and gloomy castle. Thunder and lightning crashed, and people fell off the top of the tall tower.

Pulling away from the table Shena whispered, "That's a scary card!"

"Well, dear," Madam Bonita explained, "this is the Tower card. It does tell us something quite upsetting is coming your way. But," she continued, turning over the second card, "it won't be anything you can't handle." The newly turned card pictured a large, happy sun glowing over a group of joyful children.

"In fact, I'd say that a miracle is coming your way!" she added, slipping the two cards back into the deck with the rest. As she did so, the sounds of gypsies preparing their dinners traveled over the evening breezes to Madam Bonita's tent.

"Shena, Shena where are you? It's time to get washed for supper. Sheeena!" Abruptly, Shena's mother's voice ended her visit with Madam Bonita. Thanking the fortune teller for her reading, Shena stood up and hurried to her family's bright blue wagon.

"Hurry now, honey. Wash up for supper!" her mother said, smiling. As Shena and her parents ate, the fire kindled to cook the meal dwindled to low embers.

After eating dinner and washing the dishes, Shena listened to the older gypsies tell stories by their fires. She enjoyed listening to the stories almost as much as spending time with her friend, Madam Bonita.

Climbing into her cot at bedtime, Shena didn't fall asleep right away. Instead, she lay quietly, gazing through her small, crescent-shaped window toward the sky above. As she imagined the great archer, Orion, shooting flaming arrows from his golden bow, she listened to the sweet, sad sound of one lonely gypsy violin, singing to the distant stars. Closing her eyes, Shena rode the silvery notes into safe, comfortable sleep. During the night she had only one dream. In her dream she saw a single, tall tower standing in the middle of a flower-covered meadow.

The next morning dusty sunlight danced through the window,

warming Shena's face. Fading with the stars, her dream about the tower was soon forgotten. Because it was Sunday, the gypsy camp was quiet. On Sundays townspeople go to church, to picnics and on family buggy rides instead of attending gypsy fairs. While the other gypsies spent a peaceful morning in camp, Shena gulped down breakfast and packed her swimming clothes in a small, leather bag. During his visit to the fair earlier in the week, the local minister, Reverend Brown, had invited Shena to join his family on a church picnic down by the town swimming hole. With a daughter about Shena's age, Reverend and Mrs. Brown thought the two girls would have a good time playing together.

Arriving at the gypsy camp an hour after the morning church service, which seemed a very long time past sunup to Shena, Reverend Brown stepped from his wagon and helped his wife and daughter down. Shena and her parents were on hand to greet the minister and his family. While the adults were introducing themselves, Shena and Reverend Brown's daughter stood looking shyly at each other. Neither girl said a word.

"Ruth, where are your manners?" Mrs. Brown scolded her daughter. "Say hello."

Red-faced, but unable to get out of it, Ruth held out her hand and mumbled, "Hello, Shena, nice to meet you." As soon as Ruth spoke, Shena knew that she and Ruth had something very special in common. Ruth was missing her two front teeth!

Shena smiled her very biggest smile, "Hi Ruth!" she said. When Ruth saw the gap between Shena's teeth, she smiled a great big smile right back.

"I knew they'd be friends," said Reverend Brown, grinning at Shena's parents. Helping his wife back into the wagon, he assured them he'd have their daughter home by dinner time. Climbing onto the fresh hay in the back of the minister's wagon, the two girls were soon sharing secrets and giggling happily.

"Have a good time, honey!" Shena's mother called as the wagon rolled out of the gypsy camp.

It didn't take long to arrive at the picnic grounds where Shena and Ruth tumbled out of the wagon and ran to explore the area. In the center of a large, grassy meadow, the picnic grounds lay beside a deep, clear creek which gurgled over rocks and rushed past families enjoying the pleasant, summer day.

Quickly becoming best friends, Shena and Ruth filled the cheerful, sunny hours swimming in the creek, and eating fried chicken, cold potato salad, and crisp green pickles. They even shared large helpings of peach ice cream. Happy families crowded the picnic grounds as the smell of homemade food, and the sound of laughing children, floated on warm, afternoon breezes. After savoring her second helping of ice cream, Shena plopped down and leaned back against a large oak tree.

"I'm going to swim with the other kids," Ruth announced.

"Okay, I'm gonna relax a bit, and then I'll come too," Shena replied. Planning to rest for just a few minutes, she closed her eyes and fell sound asleep.

"Hurry! Over here, Doc!" Shena woke to loud yelling. Panicked and frightened, the whole crowd of picnickers ran toward the swimming hole.

"Let him through! He's a doctor!" screamed a woman.

"Make way for the doc! Hurry, Doc!" yelled a man.

Following the group, Shena ran toward the river. A ring of adults circled someone, or something, making a wall of legs and backs. Shena could not see through, or over, the growing crowd. Glancing around quickly, she located a weeping willow tree hanging far over the creek.

Earlier in the day, the children had jackknifed into the cool waters below using the tree as a diving board. Knowing that she would be able to see more clearly from its tall branches, Shena quickly climbed the old tree. Settling on a strong branch, she parted the pale green, feather-like leaves of the willow and stared out over the crowd.

Leaning over his patient, black bag open wide at his side, the doctor blocked Shena's view of the person centered in all the excitement. Slowly, the doctor straightened and stood up. Speaking very softly, he said something to Reverend and Mrs. Brown standing nearby.

"Oh, no! God, no! Not my baby!" Mrs. Brown cried out. "No, no, no!" She wailed and sobbed. Several women wrapped their arms around her and led her away from the crowd. Shena watched as Reverend Brown leaned down and picked up the still, oh so still, person from the ground. And then, for all the world, she wished she had not climbed that tree for a better view. Reverend Brown held a wet, very pale, very limp girl. Ruth.

Taking off his coat, a man draped it over Ruth covering her entire body, even her face. Looking straight ahead, Reverend Brown carried his daughter across the meadow. Just before reaching the wagon, he turned toward the crowd of sad and frightened people.

"She's in God's hands now, brothers and sisters. Pray for her." Turning his back on the crowd, he gently laid the bundle on the straw while neighbors helped Mrs. Brown, still sobbing, into the wagon. With a soft slap of the reins, the Reverend guided the horses toward town. Sad and confused, the other picnickers soon followed. Letting the leafy cover fall, Shena wedged herself tightly into the crook of the old willow tree and wept.

In all the excitement of the tragedy, the townspeople had forgotten Shena. She didn't care if they gave her a ride home. She was so sad she didn't care if she ever climbed out of the tree. As the last wagon pulled away from the picnic grounds, Shena still sat alone, crying. Eventually her sobbing turned to sniffles. Softly, and very quietly, she began to pray for a miracle. She prayed silently, then out loud. She prayed to the God who lived in the church where the townspeople met every Sunday. She prayed to the gods and goddesses of the gypsies, and she prayed to the universal light.

"Please," she prayed, "send me a miracle!"

Sitting high in the old willow tree, Shena thought about Ruth. Letting her legs dangle over the water, she remembered the way the two of them swam and splashed each other, and how they spit watermelon seeds into the creek. Wanting Ruth back more than ever, Shena continued to pray... and pray... and pray.

Losing track of time, she hardly noticed the air turning cooler and the shadows stretching long across the meadow grass. As evening washed down the creek and splashed over the land, Shena heard the tinkling bells on the halter of her father's large horse.

"Shena! Shena girl, where are ya?" her father called.

"Here! Up here, Daddy," she answered.

"Thank the gods you're all right. When we heard of the drowning and you didn't come home... well.... everyone was very worried." Riding his horse right under the branch where Shena had spent the afternoon, her father reached up and plucked his little girl out of the tree. Kissing his daughter on the top of her head, he slid Shena into the saddle in front of him.

"Hold on tight!" he told her, "let's be gettin' home. Your mother will be havin' a fit!" Slapping the reins, he urged the big horse into a gallop and headed toward the gypsy camp.

By the time Shena and her father arrived home, dinner was bubbling in heavy iron pots hung over open fires. The fragrance of stew and baking biscuits floated through the gypsy camp. Despite the delicious smells, Shena wasn't hungry. After telling her parents all about her day, she went straight to bed. Warm and dry in her little cot, she could hear the gypsies outside her family's wagon, joking and laughing while they prepared for dinner. As twinkling stars gathered in the evening sky, she prayed, again, for a miracle. Continuing to pray until the moon was high over the wagon, she slipped into deep sleep.

"Shena? Shena! Can you hear me, you sleepy head?" Hearing her friend's voice, Shena opened her eyes. Sitting at the end of her bed, Ruth smiled playfully.

"What!" Shena sat up quickly. "I thought you drowned. You're alive! My miracle!"

"Not exactly," Ruth answered. "I did drown. But, don't worry," she said, seeing the look of dismay creeping over Shena's face, "I'm all right. In fact, I'm doing really great! I've met lots of new friends, and tomorrow I'm taking flying lessons with some angels!"

"I'm confused," said Shena, tears beginning to brim in her eyes.

"Well, I don't exactly understand it yet," Ruth went on, "but, I'm fine. Honest! And that's why I came here. To tell you I'm all right! Don't cry for me. Really. I'm okay, and I'm happy."

"Are you going to stay here?" sniffled Shena.

"No, I told you," Ruth said impatiently, "I have flying lessons with the angels tomorrow!"

"But... but," Shena stuttered, "I prayed for you to be alive again. I prayed for a miracle!"

"Oh, yes. A miracle." Ruth twisted the ends of her hair as she talked. "Well, maybe I can send you a miracle. But, I've gotta go now. Tell everyone I'm safe and I'm happy!" Ruth smiled and then seemed to fade away until Shena couldn't see anything but darkness. Listening carefully, all she could hear was her father snoring behind the curtain that separated her parents' cot from the rest of the wagon.

Shaking her head, and thinking she must have been dreaming, Shena snuggled back under her covers and fell into a very deep sleep.

At the first break of day, as the gypsies packed their wagons to move to another town, Shena ran to tell Madam Bonita about her dream. She also wanted to ask if a miracle had happened in the town during the night.

"Madam Bonita. Madam Bonita!" she called, rounding a corner. "Was there a miracle last night? Is Ruth okay?"

Popping her head out of her wagon window, Madam Bonita beckoned to Shena. "Come in, Shena. I'm getting ready to travel. We can talk as I work."

Shena skipped up the stairs of the fortune teller's purple and gold wagon and settled on a cot covered with brightly colored blankets. Madam Bonita turned and looked at Shena thoughtfully. The gypsy woman wasn't wearing a handkerchief on her head this morning, and her curly black hair was wilder than ever. As she moved her hand to brush curls from her face, the jingling of silver bracelets filled the wagon.

"Your friend, little one," Madam Bonita said softly, sitting down next to Shena, "has died. She won't be coming back in the way you knew her. I'm sorry, my dear."

Leaning against the older gypsy, Shena sniffled. A single tear rolled down her cheek. Trying hard not to cry, she described her dream about seeing Ruth.

"I wish that dream were real," she said, looking up into the kindly face of the fortune teller, "and I really prayed for a miracle!" she added.

Suddenly, Madam Bonita's eyes grew very large, and she stared at Shena. "Smile for me, little one," she said.

"But I don't feel very happy. I feel sad."

"I know, dear, but just give me one, small smile," coaxed the gypsy. Shena smiled the biggest smile she could while feeling so sad. Gasping, Madam Bonita threw her hands into the air.

"Bless the gods!" she said, "a miracle did happen, my dear!" Reaching up, Madam Bonita took a polished copper pan from a hook on the wall of her wagon.

"Look," she said, holding the shiny pan in front of Shena. "Now smile!" she commanded. Shena saw the reflection of her sad face and smiled half-heartedly.

"No, a big smile!" the gypsy woman said. Thinking that Madam Bonita was acting rather strangely, Shena looked into the pan and gave a quick smile. Instantly, she froze. There, smiling in the coppery mirror, was a little gypsy girl with a mouth full of very straight teeth. The gap could not be seen!

Running her tongue along the inside of her mouth, Shena checked her teeth. The gap really had disappeared. Each tooth lined up neatly, forming a very straight row.

"What? What happened?" she stuttered, looking back and forth from her friend's face to her own image in the pan.

"Why, a miracle, honey!" the woman said. "Your prayers were answered!"

"But, I wanted Ruth to return. That's the miracle I wanted!" Shena fought to hold back her tears.

Madam Bonita lowered the pan to the cot and held the little girl gently in her arms. Whispering softly she said, "my dear, miracles come in all shapes and sizes. They come in all sorts of disguises. Sometimes we miss miracles that are truly wonderful because we are expecting something different. What's important to know is that your prayers are being heard, and they are being answered! And, it's important for you to know that the miracles you receive are sent with love and that they are always in your best interest. Maybe your friend did have something to do with this miracle. Wasn't she missing her two front teeth?"

Drying her eyes on the sleeve of her dress, Shena sat up. "You know, I forgot. But that's how we got to be friends in the first place. And, in my dream she did say she'd try to send me a miracle. Maybe my teeth growing together is a going away present from Ruth!"

The fortune teller smiled gently. "Well, honey, maybe so. In any case, it certainly is a miracle! Now you have to run along or I won't have my wagon packed by the time we get rolling."

"Oh, thank you, Madam Bonita, for helping me to see my miracle!" Giving the fortune teller a hug, Shena turned and hurried out of the wagon. Running back to her family's wagon, she flashed big, loving smiles, sharing her miracle with every gypsy she saw along the way.

Fool's Dream: Number Two

Where Fool's magical bag plants a seed.

Jingle, jingle, jingle, the old bear heard the faint music of the fortune teller's bracelets tinkling through his sleep. Then, as softly as the dream had begun, it slipped away. Grunting and rolling over, the large bear pushed into Fool. Sound asleep, Fool shifted out of the bear's way. As he moved, he stretched his leg, kicking his staff as it leaned against the cave wall. The staff trembled for a moment, then tipped over and slid to the floor, landing with a thud. The leather bag tied to the end of Fool's staff fell open.

POOF! A sparkley cloud of magical dust puffed from the bag and drifted onto Fool. If he had been awake, and had been looking closely, he would have noticed that what appeared to be specks of dust, were really millions of tiny seeds. Shining in two shades of blue and one shade of brilliant green, the tiny seeds smelled a bit like ocean, somewhat like deep, musky jungles, and a great deal like fresh baked bread.

Landing gently on the tip of Fool's nose, one of the seeds slipped into his dreams and began to grow. This is the dream that grew from the magical seed that came from the bag that held the memory of all things past, and all things yet to come.

61

Seventh Son

Chapter Four

Seventh Son

"It's a boy! It's a boy!" Loud cries rang through the sleepy Irish village. Pushing and shoving, a ragtag crowd of villagers, holding their lanterns and smoky torches high, stumbled through the streets toward the tiny house of Nolan and Mary O'Reilly.

Shouting, cheering, and clapping, the noisy crowd broke the stillness of the dark, early morning. Several women wept and a man beat a tin pan, while a trio of noisy dogs moved along with the crowd, barking and yapping.

"It's a boy! It's a boy!"

Mary O'Reilly had just given birth to her seventh child. Each of the six other children born to the O'Reillys had been boys, making this tiny male child their seventh son. Nolan O'Reilly was also the seventh child born to a family of six boys. That meant that this new child, Finbar O'Reilly, was the seventh son of the seventh son of an Irishman.

"Mother!" cried a young girl, pulling on her mother's skirts as they hurried along with the crowd. "Mother, why is everyone so excited? Why are we running through town to the O'Reilly's house in the wee hours of the morning?"

Reaching down and taking her daughter's small hand, the woman explained. "There is a legend in Ireland, Darling. A legend that goes way, way back to the beginning of time. According to that ancient tale, the seventh son born of a seventh son in an Irish family will have the gift of healing. With his hands, this wee one will be able to heal illness, disease, and even broken hearts. So, you see, my dearest, that's why we're so excited about the newly born boy! Come now, maybe we can see the babe!" Smiling, mother and daughter hurried, hand in hand, through the town.

Huffing and puffing, Mayor Flannery, jolly, round and red-faced, led the motley crowd through winding streets of the village to the home of the O'Reilly family. Arriving at the small cottage, he banged on the door with his walking stick.

Exhausted from assisting his wife with the birth, Nolan opened the door a crack. Grinning wearily, he announced what the crowd already knew. "It's a boy! Mother and child are doing fine, but they're very tired, and we should let them sleep."

"Let us see the boy! Let us see him, *now!*" demanded the crowd.

Mopping sweat from his brow with a crumpled handkerchief, Mayor Flannery agreed with the villagers. "They're right, Nolan. Everyone has waited a long, long time for a healer to come to our village. They have a right to see him, you know."

"But," began Nolan, "both of them are totally exhausted, and they're resting. Can't you wait until the light of day?" Insisting on seeing the baby, yelling and stomping their feet and holding their torches high, the villagers continued to make a terrible racket.

"It's all right, darlin'," Mary O'Reilly called in a sweet, tired voice, "let them come to see the babe. Only ask them to hush. He's just a wee one, and the noise frightens him!"

Humbly removing their hats and lowering their heads, the villagers quietly formed a long line. First to enter, Mayor Flannery wiped his feet on the mat in the entry way and reverently approached mother and child.

Lit only by a small flame in the fireplace and a smelly oil lamp, the cottage was dark and smoky. Lining the wall opposite Mary and the newborn, two rows of bunk beds held the six other O'Reilly boys. In the first row, Timmy hung over the top of his bunk whispering to Jimmy below. Sheridan, in the bunk under Jimmy, rested on his elbows watching the activity on the other side of the room. Matthew, in the lower bunk of the second row, lay on his back, pushing up on the bottom of Mark's bed. Above him, Mark punched at the little mound in his mattress created by his brother's feet. Rodney, on the top bunk, lay sound asleep. Thoroughly enjoying all the activity, the boys were delighted with the newest addition to the family. Although they didn't exactly understand what was going on, they felt sure their new baby brother was going to be a source of entertainment for some time to come.

Hat in hand, Mayor Flannery approached the bed and gazed shyly at the infant. Chubby-cheeked, pink and round, the baby cooed contentedly in Mary O'Reilly's arms. Lying against thick goose feather pillows under a warm, downy quilt, she looked small, pale and very tired. Smiling wearily, Mary greeted the mayor by name.

After viewing mother and child, Mayor Flannery stood off in one corner of the room with Nolan O'Reilly and watched the villagers shuffle by in single file. One by one the people came through the little cottage, quietly staring at the baby.

On leaving, the villagers didn't go directly home. They remained standing outside in small groups discussing the wonderful, magical healing child who had come to their town.

While the crowd milled around in the O'Reilly's front yard, the last of the villagers, a young widow and her son, John, moved toward the house. Dragging a twisted leg, the young boy awkwardly and painfully pulled himself along. His right hand gripped a crutch, his left clutched a wooden carving of a leprechaun.

Small and whimsical, the wooden leprechaun had a round belly, a long full beard, bushy eyebrows, ears that stuck out quite a way (for listening to secrets), a pointed hat, and little leather boots with wide, square buckles. Tiny black eyes twinkled as he smiled both sweetly and mischievously. The leprechaun carving was John's gift to the new baby.

When John was six, he'd climbed high into the tip top branches of a very tall tree in his front yard. Trying to scamper like a squirrel, he'd slipped and fallen to the ground. The bone he broke in his leg had refused to set properly, leaving it twisted, and leaving John in need of his crutch.

Enraged by her son's fall from the tree and helpless to change what had already happened, John's mother turned her feelings on the tree and chopped it to the ground in anger. A neighborly furniture maker carved John's crutch from that very tree, then neatly stacked the remaining pieces of wood behind his shop. Because John could no longer run and play with the other children, he spent a great deal of time with the furniture maker learning to whittle. The branches from John's climbing tree were perfect for carving small statues of animals and leprechauns.

Leprechauns are tiny, magical beings who live in forests and valleys in the lush green land of Ireland. They love to play tricks on humans, teasing them and making them look foolish. But leprechauns are also sources of good luck. It is not unusual on the Emerald Isle to hear stories of people who've found pots brimming with gold and jewels after rescuing a leprechaun from misfortune.

Urging her son along, the woman whispered, "Hurry, John. Maybe, when the child is older, he will be able to heal your leg, and you won't need your crutch anymore."

Only a step ahead of his mother, John moved slowly and painfully, taking one step, then lifting himself along with his crutch. Another painful step, another lift with the crutch. With each step, his crutch banged sharply on the hard floor.

"Your hat, boy!" scolded Mayor Flannery. "Mind your manners!"

Blushing, John slumped on his crutch, reached up quickly, and snatched his cap from his head. The infant, lying wide awake in Mary's arms, watched John's every movement. Balancing carefully, John leaned close and said softly, "Mam, I've brought the child a gift. It's a wee leprechaun I carved from my tree. Could I be givin' it to the babe?"

Mary looked across the room toward her husband. Catching her glance, Nolan shrugged and rolled his eyes.

"Oh, I should think it would be all right. We'll have to watch that he doesn't put it in his mouth. He seems more, well..." she looked again toward her husband as if searching for the way to explain the magical properties already apparent in this tiny infant, "more advanced than most babes. But, don't worry. I'll keep an eye out. What a kind thing for you to do, John."

Bending low, John knelt over the bed and offered the carving to the baby. Gurgling and blowing silky bubbles, the fat little baby reached up with chubby fingers, grasped the carving, and touched John. As tiny fingers wrapped round John's thumb, a small spark of light jumped from the baby to John's hand.

"Oh! OUCH!" yelled John, pulling his hand away and jumping back in surprise. His crutch clattered to the floor. "Ow! That's hot!"

He hopped around the small room, his thumb in his mouth.

Gaping at John, the mayor and Nolan stood frozen. John's mother gasped, "John, son, what are you doing?"

"Licking my thumb, Mom," John answered. "I think the wee babe burned me!"

"No, not that, son! Look you're jumpin' and hoppin' about! And, and... you're not ...."

Suddenly John understood what his mother was saying. He stood fully upright in the middle of the floor while his crutch lay abandoned. John looked down at his legs. Sure enough they were straight and strong.

Cooing and gurgling, the very special baby clapped his fat little hands.

Watching the amazing scene from their beds, Timmy and Jimmy shouted out loud, "Baby is a healer! Baby is a healer!" Sheridan dove under his covers to hide while Matthew started clapping his hands and kicking his feet even harder on the bottom of Mark's bunk. Mark hung over the side of his bed and waved his fist in pretend menace at his brother's feet. Rodney continued to sleep soundly.

"Holy Mother!" cried the mayor, finally able to move. "He really is the healer. The babe is the healer!"

Rushing out the door, the mayor called to the crowd. "Look at this!" he shouted, pushing John through the door. As John walked into the yard, the villagers drew back in amazement.

"Here, Father Patrick!" Mayor Flannery shouted to the local priest. "Catch!" He tossed the crutch high in the air. As the crutch moved through space, time seemed to slow down. Just as the crutch arched and began to fall toward the waiting hands of Father Patrick, the first rays of sunlight edged from behind a cloud, streamed through the sky, and bathed the crutch in gold. Suspended in silence for a single moment, the crutch shimmered with golden light.

A loud cry went up from the crowd as Father Patrick caught the crutch. "Praise the Lord! He has given us His gift of healing!"

"Follow me, Brethren!" shouted the priest. "We must go to the church to give thanks to our Heavenly Father!" Holding the crutch high, Father Patrick led the crowd through the village streets, leaving the amazed O'Reilly family to rest, and to consider all that had happened on that early spring morning.

The news of the healer spread quickly through the Isles of Britain, and beyond. All around the globe people heard the story of the seventh son of the seventh son of the Irishman, the child healer. People traveled many miles to see young Finbar and to have his chubby hands touch and heal them. True healers never ask for payment, but people were thankful for their newfound wellness and they often brought homemade gifts of food, woven blankets, pottery and flowers. One time, a farmer offered three fat stewing chickens to Finbar's mother. Another time, a grateful woman knit sweaters for Finbar and his six brothers. Almost every week, someone new found his way to the O'Reilly home, asking for a healing from Finbar.

Despite his great healing powers, Finbar grew and played just like all the other children in the village. Racing his friends down country lanes, he sometimes won first place and sometimes came in hopelessly behind. He pulled girls' pigtails in class and then looked angelically at his teachers with a 'who, me?' expression. Fishing in the icy streams of the forest behind his village, he shared the same childhood dreams and fears as children in towns and villages all over Ireland.

But there was one thing, besides his healing power, that Finbar didn't share with the other children. His wooden leprechaun. Finbar carried the small carving in his pocket, taking it everywhere. When other folks were around, the leprechaun stayed hidden in Finbar's pocket, cleverly disguised as a fanciful wooden statue. But when they were alone, the leprechaun sprang to life! Wriggling out of the pocket, he often hopped on Finbar's shoulder, offering stories, rhymes and even an occasional joke or two. Finbar and the leprechaun were inseparable friends.

One bright, sunny afternoon, as Finbar skipped happily down the road to purchase eggs for the next morning's breakfast, he noticed a man about the same age as his own father just outside the gates of a neighboring village. The man's right leg hung withered, and twisted, and he leaned against a crutch. Holding a dented tin cup, the man called out to each passerby. "Alms. Alms," he said in a thin, pathetic voice. "Alms for a poor beggar. Alms for a cripple." Finbar had never seen this behavior.

"Sir," he said, walking up to the man, "what are you doing?"

The beggar glanced at Finbar. "I'm begging, of course. Do you have any money you can give me?" Finbar thought about the egg money.

"I have some money, sir," he answered, "but I have to use it all to buy eggs. I'm on an errand for my mother."

"Oh," said the man, rather gruffly, "well, be moving along then. Alms. Alms for the poor," he called as a carriage rolled by, "alms for a cripple."

Finbar didn't leave.

"Be gone boy!" the beggar snarled at Finbar, "you're standin' in my spot."

"Well, sir," Finbar smiled widely, "this is your lucky day!"

"What do you mean?" asked the beggar, not paying much attention to Finbar. "Did you find some extra money in your pocket?"

"No," Finbar answered, "but, I'm a healer. I'll cure that leg for you. You won't have to stand here any more, expecting money from others."

"What?" asked the man, spinning around on his crutch in surprise. "What do you mean you can fix my leg?" Squinting his eyes he looked at Finbar suspiciously.

"It's easy," Finbar responded. "All I have to do is touch people who are ill or crippled, or even feeling really sad, and they are well! I... I don't know how it works," he went on, "but I've been doing it all my life."

"Nobody can help me!" said the man harshly.

"I can," nodded Finbar eagerly, "in fact, when I was just a wee babe, I reached out and touched a boy with a leg as crippled as yours. Today he's a strong young farmer with sons of his own. I can heal you, too!" Beaming, Finbar extended his hand toward the beggar.

"No, stop!" shouted the man, alarmed. "You stay away from me! I'm just fine the way I am. I've been doing this all my life. Leave me alone!"

"But... what do you mean?" asked Finbar, clearly confused. "I can help you!"

"Stay away!" shouted the man. "I told you, nobody can help me. Now, go away!"

"But... but... your life. I can help you change your life. I can heal you. You won't be crippled any more."

"I told you to go away!" yelled the man, now clearly very angry. "I don't want to change. Not for you or anybody else. Now get out of here!"

Staring in disbelief, Finbar continued trying to convince the beggar. "You must just be afraid of how it feels when I touch you. It's just a tiny shock, nothing really. Here, let me just brush your hand. You'll be so happy you did!" Finbar pleaded, stretching out his healing hands toward the man.

"No!" yelled the man. Raising his crutch in the air he sent it crashing down hard on Finbar's hands.

"OW!" shrieked Finbar.

Turning quickly, the beggar hobbled away in the opposite direction.

"OW!" cried Finbar again, sobbing with pain. "My hands, my hands hurt so much!" Forgetting the eggs, Finbar began running back to his village as fast as he could go. By the time he reached his family's cottage, his hands were red and swollen. Large dark welts puffed up along the tops of his fingers. Bursting through the cottage door, he ran directly to his mother.

Seeing her son upset, she stopped stirring dinner and bent to hug him. "There, there, little one. You're safe now. There, there. Mother's here. What's the matter?"

Although he didn't know why, Finbar felt slightly ashamed by what had happened with the beggar. Instead of telling his mother the truth, he made up a tale.

"Oh, Mother. I... I tripped on a rock and fell. I smacked my hands hard... on the ground." He'd never lied to his mother before, and suddenly Finbar felt terrible.

"Well, now, don't you worry," his mother lovingly consoled him, "go to the bucket and wash with cold water. That will help. You'll feel better after dinner. We're having your favorite, mutton stew!"

Finbar hardly touched his stew. He felt bad about lying to his mother, and his fingers continued to sting with pain. "Mother," he said, "this stew is good, but I don't feel like eating tonight. I just want to go to bed."

"Of course, son," she answered, "there'll be plenty left over, and you can have some for lunch tomorrow." Pushing in his chair, Finbar left the table and slipped into his little bunk bed against the wall. Before long, the rest of the family finished dinner, and were soon tucked away safely in their beds, sound asleep.

KNOCK! KNOCK! KNOCK! The loud noise on their front door woke Finbar's family.

"Help!" cried the voice of an old man. "Bring the healer, my wife's taken sick! We need your help!" Finbar, used to being called to heal in the middle of the night, whispered loudly across the room to his parents behind their curtain. "It's okay. I'll go with him." Dressing quickly, he headed out the cabin door.

"Be safe!" called his mother, as Finbar slipped into the night air.

"Hurry, son," the villager said. "I think she's taken a bad cough. Our cabin is way down by the forest; we'll have to hurry." Finbar and the old man moved briskly through the darkened village and along the road toward the forest. Arriving a short while later, the man led Finbar into his cabin and over to his wife's bed. A pale, very thin old woman coughed loudly. Closing his eyes, and reaching out his hands, Finbar took a deep breath and touched the woman's throat and forehead.

Nothing.

Absolutely nothing happened. No spark. No feelings of relief for the woman. Nothing.

Another fit of coughing began. "I... I don't know what's wrong," Finbar stuttered, looking back and forth from the old man to his sick wife.

"Try again, boy," the man pleaded.

Taking another deep breath, Finbar closed his eyes and placed his hands on the woman again.

Nothing. Nothing at all. "Oh, sir. I'm so sorry. I... I hurt my hands yesterday and maybe..."

"Come with me, boy," said the old man quietly. Draping his arm over Finbar's shoulders, he shuffled toward the door of the cabin. "Maybe, son," he whispered softly, "maybe it's not for her to be healed. Maybe it's God's will that she leave now. You tried, and I thank you for that." Choking back a tear, the man asked Finbar if he needed help finding his way home.

"No, no, I'm all right. I... I'm so sorry," he whispered as the man slowly closed the cabin door.

Hanging his head in confusion and sadness, Finbar began the long walk home.

As the first rays of sun splashed over the lush, Irish hillsides, Finbar heard a noisy commotion in the distance. Curious, he ran to the source of the noise and found a small crowd of people huddled around a young man sitting on the ground.

"Can you move it, Tommy?" a young woman asked fearfully.

"No, lass. It hurts too much," he winced.

"Look, it's the healer!" an onlooker called out, noticing Finbar approaching. "Healer, come help us! Tommy O'Hart's fallen from his horse and broken his leg. Come heal him!"

Finbar hurried to the young man. Kneeling beside Tommy, he closed his eyes, and reaching out his hand, laid it very gently on the fellow's leg.

Nothing. Nothing at all. Just as with the old woman, no spark, no feeling, no relief. Nothing.

"Well, do it, boy," said Tommy through gritted teeth.

"I... I..." stuttered Finbar, turning a bright red. Lowering his hands to Tommy's leg, he tried sending healing energy. But again, nothing happened.

"Better go fetch the doctor, Molly," a bystander said to the young woman beside Tommy, "the healer seems to be havin' a bad day, or somethin'." The villagers turned their attention away from Finbar to the injured Tommy O'Hart.

Confused and embarrassed, Finbar stood up, turned and began sprinting from the crowd. Instead of heading toward his home, he took the road leading into the forest. Running until his lungs almost burst, he sobbed out loud.

Completely out of breath, with very sore legs and eyes swollen from crying, Finbar finally stopped running. Finding himself deep within the forest, he sat down on a rotting log at the edge of the path. Catching his breath, Finbar felt a familiar wriggling from his pocket as the leprechaun popped out and hopped up on a clump of mushrooms growing out of the log.

"This is no time to be hoppin' about," Finbar sniffed angrily.

"Oh, now. Something goin' wrong for our wee lad?" asked the leprechaun, raising his bushy eyebrows. "Tell me all about it," he said, settling comfortably on the top of the largest mushroom.

Finbar glumly shared all that had happened in the past two days. "So, you see," he said, finishing his story, "now, I really can't go home. Not only did I lie to my mother, but I can't heal folks anymore. I'll have to run away and keep running."

Sighing, Finbar lowered his head to his hands.

"Now, just a minute, lad," reprimanded the leprechaun. "Just because you're a healer..."

"WAS a healer!" interrupted Finbar.

"AH HEM!" Clearing his throat, the leprechaun went on. "As I was sayin', just because you WERE a healer, doesn't mean you

know all the answers. What happened to you was a lesson."

"A lesson?" Finbar said, confused. "What's a lesson?"

"Life, my boy," began the leprechaun, "is full of lessons. We are constantly given opportunities to learn them. Sometimes we learn what we're supposed to. Other times, we don't."

"What happens if we don't learn our lessons?" asked Finbar, more interested.

"Simple," shrugged the leprechaun. "We just get another opportunity. Most of the time it's much, much easier to learn our lessons the first time around. You'd be surprised," giggled the leprechaun impishly, "how many folks need to try over, and over, and over again to get even the simplest learning!"

"Well," wondered Finbar, slowly, "just what lesson did I learn?"

"Oh, that," said the leprechaun seriously, "well, you learned one of the hardest lessons of all. You learned not all people want help, or healing. You simply can't 'fix' everyone."

"But," interrupted Finbar again, "but, I could have helped that beggar! I could have healed him. I could have changed his life for the better!"

"Maybe not," answered the leprechaun, "and that's the lesson. You see, lad, in this life, the best we can do is to love and heal ourselves. Then we can reach out and love and heal those who want our help. People have a choice. They may change their lives if they want to. It's our job to help them, but only if they really want change. And only if they ask for our help. People have to make up their own minds whether or not they want to heal."

"I still don't understand," mused Finbar, thoughtfully. "If the man could be healed, and his life would change for the better, why didn't he want my help?"

"Well, lad. First off, you don't really know how healing would have changed his life. We'll probably never know. More importantly, that beggar didn't want help. Period. That's his choice. It's his right.

We don't have the right to interfere."

Sitting in silence, Finbar and the leprechaun stared out into the leafy green forest. Sunlight filtered through the branches of tall trees, making shifting patterns on the thick forest floor. Tiny white flowers dotted soft mounds of lime green moss. Bright orange toadstools and mushrooms stood at attention. Small chickadees squabbled in the boughs of a tree off in the distance, and a large, round-eyed jay sat on a low branch, staring at the leprechaun, listening to every word he said.

Finbar sighed. "You know," he said softly, "I seem to be having a problem with my hands. And, I lied to my mother. I can feel that in my heart." Looking directly at his friend sitting quietly on the mushroom, he said, "Leprechaun, I'd like my hands to be healed. I'd like some help."

"Well, okay then!" smiled the leprechaun, slapping his thigh and jumping up. Balancing on the top of the slippery fungus, he reached into his tiny pocket and brought out a handful of gold dust. "Close your eyes!" he commanded. Finbar shut his eyes tightly. "Be Well, and Blessed Be!" shouted the leprechaun, flinging the sparkling dust over Finbar.

Opening his eyes, Finbar looked around. "Did... did it work?" he asked.

"Of course it worked!" laughed the leprechaun. "Now, I'll just hop off this 'shroom and climb on your shoulder. We can spend the day exploring the forest." Starting toward the edge of the mushroom, the leprechaun lost his footing, slipped and went flying into the air. Landing with a tiny thud on the forest floor, he cried out, "Ohhhh! I twisted my ankle. Ohhh! Finbar, please help me! The pain! The pain!"

Quickly kneeling by his little friend, Finbar closed his eyes and took a deep breath. The leprechaun looked up and gave the big jay bird a sly wink.

Finbar carefully touched the leprechaun's tiny leg. SPARK! A flash of light blazed between Finbar's hand and the leprechaun's leg.

"Well, I'll be!" said the little fellow, hopping up and strutting around in circles. "Good as new!"

"Oh! Thank you!" Finbar rolled his eyes skyward. "Thank you! Now I can go home!"

"Well, now. Isn't there something you need to do when you get there?" asked the leprechaun as Finbar gently placed him on his shoulder.

"Yes, I have to go and tell my mother the truth. Then, I'll go see if Tommy O'Hart and that old woman would still like my help."

"Oh, that!" said the leprechaun, pretending to be disappointed. "I thought you were going to offer me some of that delicious, leftover stew!"

Finbar laughed and began to whistle as he walked briskly out of the forest toward home. Riding on Finbar's shoulder, the leprechaun looked back toward the big jay. The bird tilted his head and blinked at the leprechaun as if questioning the entire event. Smiling, like someone holding a secret, the leprechaun waved to the bird, then faced forward, and joined Finbar in whistling a happy, Irish jig.

Fool's Dream: Number Three

Where Grandmother Hattie spins a story.

"Geeze...." muttered Fool, waking up and stretching. "That certainly was a different sort of dream." Looking around the cave, Fool noticed the old brown bear deep in sleep with a big smile stretched across his face. Intuit lay on his back, completely upside down, for a dog, with all four legs spread wide. His paws paddled the air. "Looks like he's swimming!" Fool thought to himself, stifling a giggle. "What a silly dog!"

Tiptoeing to the edge of the cave and peeking out, Fool drew in a deep breath of cold, fresh air. A new, sweet smell mixed with the brisk winter scents. The fragrance reminded Fool of something very pleasant.

"What is that smell?" he wondered, moving quietly back to where his friends were sleeping. Trying hard to remember, Fool curled up next to the bear. "Oh, well, it will come." Snuggling close to the slumbering animals, Fool closed his eyes and began to drift off.

"SPRING!" he said out loud, sitting up quickly.

"Ugh. Ummmm," muttered the bear, not quite awake.

"Oh, sorry, Bear," whispered Fool, lying back down. "I didn't mean to wake you. It's just that I remembered that smell! It's spring! That means sunshine must be just around the corner!"

"Ughhh," the bear responded, making little sloppy noises with his tongue.

Smiling, Fool closed his eyes again. "Just a little more sleep. I just want to sleep a little longer," he thought, "then, it will be spring." Sighing softly, and grinning to himself, Fool began to slip into peaceful rest. Just on the edge of sleep, the image of Grandmother Hattie floated gently into Fool's thoughts. The kind old woman smiled lovingly at Fool and, placing her hand, very gently, over his heart, she whispered a story into his dreams. This is the story Grandmother Hattie spun for Fool as he slept, waiting for spring.

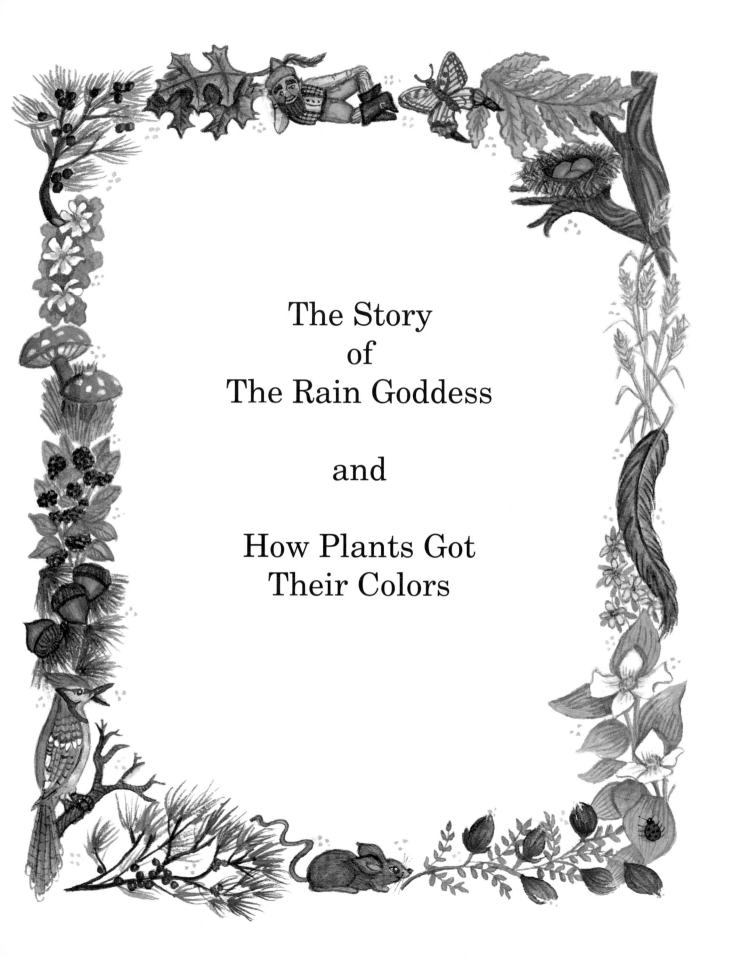

The Story
of
The Rain Goddess

and

How Plants Got
Their Colors

Chapter Five

<u>The Story of the Rain Goddess and</u>
<u>How Plants Got Their Colors</u>

Once upon a time, a long, long time ago, before people or animals came into being, only plants and gods and goddesses lived and played on Mother Earth. Mother Earth, a round, wavy, blue planet, nurtured the plants with her deep blue waters and her rich, dark soils. In those days, plants were not the color green, as we know them today. And, back then, flowers didn't have any color either. All the plants growing on Mother Earth were simply a dull, faded grayish color. However, the plants grew strong and happy, and dressed Mother Earth in a rich fabric of faded gray.

One afternoon, a group of young gods and goddesses, enjoying lunch in the clouds, peeked over the edge of their fluffy picnic area and gazed down on Mother Earth.

"Wouldn't it be lovely," mused a pretty, golden-haired goddess, "if Mother Earth were covered with a fine dress in a color different than gray?"

"Yes," agreed a handsome young god, "actually, I'm tired of looking at that same old gray. Let's ask Mother Earth to change the plants to some other color!"

Together, the gods and goddesses called down to Mother Earth.

"Mother Earth!" asked one, "won't you please change the color of the plants? That dull gray is really quite boring!"

"You are such a beautiful planet, you really deserve greater splendor!" added another.

Flattered by their attention, Mother Earth agreed. "I am a blue planet," she declared. "I will make all the plants blue, just like me!"

"Wonderful!" said a smiling young god. "We'd all love to see bright, blue plants!" Clapping and nodding, the other gods and goddesses joined in agreement.

Just as Mother Earth began to change the plants to blue, Father Sun poked his shining head from behind the puffy clouds.

"Now wait just a minute, Mother Earth!" he called down from the sky. "It's true your blue waters give the plants cool drinks, but if it weren't for my warm, yellow rays, the plants would not be nourished. They could not grow. It's sunlight that feeds all plants. Therefore," Father Sun announced loudly, "I say the plants should all be yellow, just like me!"

"You are most incorrect!" fumed Mother Earth stubbornly. "I grow the plants! They will be blue like me!" Quickly, she began pulling

the roots of the plants deep inside her to hide them from Father Sun.

"Well, I say *you* are wrong, Blue Lady Earth!" hissed Father Sun angrily. "The plants shall be yellow!" He began to shine very, very, brightly. So brightly that the plants began to burn.

The poor little plants! Pulled and tugged by Mother Earth, and scorched by Father Sun.

"Help! Help!" the frightened plants called out. "Help!"

Unaware of the ruckus happening on earth, the Rain Goddess had just begun her afternoon dance. Thought by many to be the most beautiful of all goddesses, the Rain Goddess had skin and hair the color

of silver coins. Her eyes, the deep slate of storm clouds, flashed with
brilliant sparks of white lightning. Glistening and shimmering, she
scattered silvery glitter into the air as she twirled and spun in her wild,
wet dance. Her dress, as light as silk, flowed in seven brilliant colors
across the heavens. Great chiffon ribbons of red, orange, yellow, green,
blue, indigo and magical, mystical violet twisted and floated behind the
beautiful goddess.

"Help! Help! Rain Goddess, please help us!" cried the little plants as the Rain Goddess danced high over the earth.

Pausing for a moment, the Rain Goddess looked down on the struggling plants. She knew that something was dreadfully wrong as she watched the plants beginning to disappear into Mother Earth. And, she could clearly see that instead of being fed by Father Sun, his heat toasted them!

"Whatever is going on here?" she demanded of Mother Earth and Father Sun.

"Well, it's quite obvious," whined Mother Earth, "Father Sun is ruining the plants by shining so brightly. He wants the plants to be yellow, to match him!"

"Just look at selfish Mother Earth!" sizzled Father Sun. "She's trying to hide all the plants. She wants them to be blue, just like her! Whoever heard of blue plants!" Hearing Father Sun's comment, Mother Earth pulled even harder, sucking the plants deeper into herself. Father Sun fiercely turned up his heat, burning the plants even more.

"Stop it this instant!" demanded the Rain Goddess. "If you do not stop this silly fighting, this very moment, I will not dance for either of you again! Father Sun, you will not see my shimmering dress floating across the sky. Mother Earth, I will not glide over your rivers and valleys, and you will never feel the cool step of my silver as I waltz close to your heart."

"But, Rain Goddess!" cried Mother Earth, "the other gods and goddesses want the plants to be more colorful. Father Sun and I are only trying to please them!"

"Yes, Rain Goddess," added Father Sun, "we're doing the right thing; we just can't agree on how to do it!"

"Well, compromise!" answered the Rain Goddess. "Get together and be a team! That's the best way to do any job. You both know that!"

Spinning around in disgust, she noticed the swirls of her skirt skimming the clouds behind her.

"Ah, there's the answer!" she called to Mother Earth and Father Sun. "Look at my dress." Pointing a long, slender finger toward the stream of colors behind her, she continued. "Between the blue streak of color and the bright yellow band, floats a shining ribbon of green. Give you any ideas, hmmmm?"

"Well," said Mother Earth, slowly, "I'm blue and Father Sun is yellow." Forming mountain ridges as she scrunched her face in thought, Mother Earth paused.

"Maybe," interrupted Father Sun loudly, "we could get together and make green!"

"Good idea!" smiled the Rain Goddess. "Now, stop your fighting and get to work! I'll come back tomorrow afternoon to see what you've accomplished!"

Soon, Father Sun stopped burning and Mother Earth quit pulling. They began to work together, lovingly pushing the plants skyward, and gently warming new buds into strength and growth. As they joined in their efforts, Mother Earth started to view Father Sun as gentle, strong, and quite handsome. Father Sun began to take very close notice of Mother Earth's lush, watery curves. Feeling harmony between Mother Earth and Father Sun, the little plants lost their fear and began to grow straight and tall.

The following afternoon, when the Rain Goddess arrived, all of the plants radiated a brilliant blend of bright yellow, from Father Sun, and vibrant, shining blue from Mother Earth. Fresh, bright and healthy, the little plants delighted in showing off the most beautiful shades of green ever found in the universe. Sliding across the sky, the Rain Goddess looked down at the little green plants below.

"Good work!" she nodded approvingly to Father Sun. "Wonderful job!" she called to Mother Earth. Skimming down to get a better look, her colorful, flowing, silky dress trailed behind her, brushing the face of Mother Earth. Whenever her dress touched a plant, a flower bloomed in the color of the stripe that caressed it. Moving lightly over Mother Earth, the Rain Goddess left valleys, jungles, prairies, and gardens of brightly colored flowers topping the newly deep green plants.

"Oh thank you! Thank you, Rain Goddess!" called out the little plants joyfully.

Smiling, very pleased with herself, the Rain Goddess rose high, spinning into a magnificent dance, sending buckets of silvery, glittering raindrops from the sky. The happy plants clapped and swayed below on Mother Earth. Father Sun beamed brightly, lighting the Rain Goddess's dress as it shimmered in a large, iridescent bow across the heavens.

From that day forward, Mother Earth and Father Sun found great joy working together as a team. And even today, the plants remain grateful for the help of the beautiful Rain Goddess.

"And so, my dear one," whispered Grandmother Hattie as she began to fade from Fool's dream, "whenever you see a rainbow floating across the sky, look at the flowers and plants on Mother Earth. You will find them bright and extremely happy. And if you look very carefully, through the sparkling raindrops, you will see the flowers bowing and waving to the Rain Goddess as she shimmers and dances in the heavens above."

Spring

Where Fool, Intuit, and the old brown bear
start something new.

Dreaming of the Rain Goddess and brightly colored flowers, Fool heard the plop, plop, plopping of snow melting from the outside roof of the cave. Drip. Drip. Drip. He heard drops of fresh clear water splashing on moist, dark earth. Rainbow dreams began to fade as the sounds and smells of springtime became more clear. Slowly, and very gently, Fool opened his eyes. A single ray of bright sunlight shot across the cave, landed on Intuit's face and tickled the sleeping dog's nose.

"Uff. Ummm. Ruff." Intuit snorted. "CHOO!" Sneezing, he woke with a start and stared at Fool.

"Good morning, good boy!" Fool grinned at his buddy. Intuit's tail began to wag in circles faster and faster as he reached up and happily licked Fool's face.

"Yucky!" laughed Fool, hugging the squirming dog.

"Hey, Bear!" Fool called. "Wake up, sleepy head!"

"Uff. Ummm. Ahhhh." The bear yawned a huge, wide-mouthed yawn. Making small slurping noises, he opened one eye and squinted at Fool.

"Springtime, already?" he asked, yawning again.

"Yes, bear! It's spring! Wake up! Wake up!" Fool teased. Standing up for a big stretch, he noticed his open bag and his staff, lying on the floor. Bending over to tie and close the bag, the memory of a land far, far away flitted through Fool's thoughts.

"Bear," he asked, "have you ever seen a leprechaun?"

"No," mumbled the bear, scratching behind one ear. "Why?"

"Oh, no reason," Fool answered. "Must have been something I dreamed. Never mind." Walking toward the door of the cave, he turned and called to Intuit.

"C'mon, boy! Let's go outside!" Intuit stretched, facing downward with his rump high in the air, his tail in waving circles. Yawning, he stretched again, this time with his nose pointing high. Bounding to the door of the cave, he startled a blue jay sitting on a fir tree just outside. As the bird fluttered upward, Intuit had a brief memory of another, very large bird. A bird with a rubbery, blue neck. But the memory melted quickly as the little dog bounced out of the cave into the bright spring morning.

Shuffling slowly behind his friends, the old bear began to think about where he would travel during the spring and summer.

"Hmmm, maybe I'll head over the mountain to the old gypsy campgrounds," he mumbled to himself, "just to see what I can see." Scratching his ear again, he joined Fool and Intuit outside.

While Fool and the old brown bear blinked in the bright yellow sunlight, Intuit jumped up and down and danced round in circles barking joyfully. Seeing a squirrel scurry through the trees, he took off running, filled with energy and joy.

"Feel better after your nap?" asked the bear as he began shuffling toward the trees.

"Much better! Much, much better!" smiled Fool. Overhead, puffy white clouds floated lazily across the crisp, blue sky. Following Intuit and the old brown bear, Fool skipped along, whistling a silly tune. Rested and happy, the three friends headed into the forest in search of blueberries, butterflies and brand new adventures.